AHZ-MUND'S
WRATH

– VOLUME I –

by Maddoc Rex Deacon

(1st Edition)

Copyright 2024

ISBN: 979-8-9903096-0-9

This one goes out to the strugglers and the dreamers out there; the many loners that sit in their rooms and wonder what could be out there and what the future holds for them; the black sheep, the strays, the wallflowers, the misfits, and everyone else that this world has cast out. *There is still a chance.* Go out and make it all happen. No one can truly be the best; **just have fun with it.**

Table of Contents

It is said that old dogs can't learn new tricks.....

Umbral Exordium

In a dense blanket of endless, misty midnight, the climax of an ancient, desperate conflict had come to a close. The survivors now flee in the vain hopes that they might escape the oppressive, iron grip of the victor—a necromancer with nearly endless reach. His tireless and vastly-numbered undead armies conquered and consumed all in their wake, leaving the survivors as the very last of the living in the entirety of their universe.....

All was still. Then, the black mist that filled the spaces between the kilns of radiance and the floating plateaus began to contort and swirl as it gave way to an enormously large craft—a stone brick battleship that resembled a castle which was being propelled forward by a blast furnace of a turbine engine, spewing out flames as it gushed smoke into the mist. Two smaller versions of the same craft joined the lead one moments later.

Then, out from behind the three ships came an even larger shape—a gigantic, five-fingered skeletal hand. Then, the rest of it followed, pushing apart the billowing black mist to reveal the fullness of its form. It was a floating ribcage with arms, and it defied all sense of logic as it moved forward without any sort of propulsion system, seemingly powered by some sort of foul, umbral magic. Its hands reached outwards to the battleships, as though hoping to snatch them up in its grasp. Out from behind the ribcage came dozens more just like it. Then, hundreds and thousands more appeared. Soon enough, there were millions, all of which were bearing down on the three surviving craft.

Inside the stone-walled command cabin of the *Artoum*, the lead battleship, plate-armored Guardsmen and robed Tech-Mages were sweating bullets as waves of panic overtook them. Grey Phaselight, Dire Magistral of the Guardsmen, stared with widened hazel eyes that pulsed with fear as he watched the encroaching menagerie of madness on a magic-powered view screen. His salt-and-pepper hair was matted to his forehead, and the armor that he had been wearing for several days straight had started to chafe against his skin. On his back, he wore a black cape emblazoned with the sigil of a bow-wielding sentinel using a sword as an arrow.

"Dire Magistral!" one of the Tech-Mages called out to him from behind. Grey turned around to face a weary-looking Elder Mage Francis, who was dressed in golden robes. The man's hair and long beard were stark white, a sign of his old age, and his tired brown eyes had long lost their luster over the course of the dreaded, life-long war they had seen. "We need more time! We haven't cracked it yet, but I'm sure we can uncover the secret of how the weapon operates and use it against our foe!" Elder Mage Francis said with fear creeping into his aged voice.

"Time is not on our side this day, Elder Francis. If your Mages can't crack it, then..." responded the Dire Magistral. "Then, what will we do?!" Elder Mage Francis cried. Grey thought this over for a moment, then his eyes narrowed as his expression took on a more determined look, and he said: "We will have to try something else. If the *Geleur* were able to fight off the *Unwilling*, slow their advance, and trap the necromancer, then there must be a way."

He then moved quickly past Francis and the other Mages, who stood shoulder-to-shoulder in a circular formation and hurriedly busied themselves with a strange cube made up of alien technological components. "If all else fails, secure the *assets!*" the Dire Magistral ordered as he walked.

Grey then entered the open, stone-doored elevator, which closed together after he pressed in one of the runic symbols on a control panel inside it. Then, the elevator began to lower at a slow rate, and Grey could hear the unnerving noises of the encroaching enemy's boney makeup outside the ship while the automatic pulley system of the elevator whined and squealed. Soon enough, the box containing Grey settled into place with a firm shake before its doors reopened, revealing a storage room that held a bountiful variety of strange artifacts that had a matching aesthetic to one another.

Grey entered the room and walked past two coffin-like stone boxes that had glowing white runes inscribed upon them. Though they bore a similar patterning to the ones that the Guardsmen and Tech-Mages used, the glowing runes were far more ancient and worn in appearance, as were the boxes themselves. Grey strolled right past these and towards a bundled-up collection of what looked like very long bricks of stone decorated with an old rune at their top and quickly retrieved one before returning to the elevator and pressing in another one of the runic symbols on its interior panel.

Once back inside, he grabbed ahold of the top of the brick and pulled it off, spilling dust at his feet and revealing the handle of a sword that appeared to have not been touched for centuries underneath. It was gleaming and pristine, and not a speck of rust was upon its metal. Dropping the top of the brick in the lantern-lit interior of the elevator, Grey then wrapped his hand around the object and drew it out, revealing a sword with a small, orange gem set into its curved guard and a long blade with a wire-like runic design etched into it.

Taken by its beauty, Grey took a moment to look the weapon over as he held it in his hands, letting the stone brick that housed it fall away to the floor of the rising elevator, reducing the sheath-like object to a fine powder. Then, the lift came to a stop and its stone doors reopened to showcase the sight of the enormous craft's top deck. The black mist that populated the open air tasted earthy and full of minerals as it swirled about the fleeing craft and past the Dire Magistral's face. Grey stepped out onto the brick laid path that led to gargantuan stone towers, and ahead of him was the largest of the towers, which he kicked up into a run towards.

As he ran, Grey lifted his armored wrist up to his face and spoke into a glowing rock affixed to it with string. "Any luck yet?!" he yelled as he continued moving. "No, sir, nothing yet!" the voice of Elder Mage Francis came in clearly from out of the wrist-rock, sounding ethereal and otherworldly due to the magick that powered it. "Alright, well keep at it!" Grey shouted into the large gem. After running at full speed across the ship's top for a time, Grey eventually arrived at the large tower and threw open its large, double wooden doors.

Once inside, he took a breath in before racing up its spiral staircase towards its top. "Come on, come on!" he muttered loudly to himself as he ran. Once he was near the tower's top, Grey looked out through one of the slit-like windows in its circular walls, where he could see the necromancer's forces encroaching upon the Guardsmen's ship in the far-off darkness. He then continued to run up the stone stairs until reaching the top of the tower's interior. In the center of the floor was a strange altar that stood beneath the square-shaped opening above him, which revealed the sights of the outside world to him. Grey looked the weapon over and then turned his eyes to the altar, which had a slit-like opening at its top that appeared to have just enough space in it to fit the blade of the sword.

"Ah, I see now..." Grey muttered again to himself. Placing the longsword into the slot, Grey could feel a surge of power building within the altar, and soon enough, the small gem embedded in the weapon's guard started to take on a blindingly bright glow that caused him to shield his eyes.

When he reached forward to try and grasp it once more, Grey was sent flying back against the wall of the tower's top, and a wave of pain shot through him like electricity. A blast of energy fired up and out of the square opening of the tower before dispersing in a random and jagged fashion much like stray bolts of lightning in a storm.

The bolts seared into the legions of giant ribcages, managing to burn away a small number of them to ash. Grey cried out as he curled up into a ball and cradled his arm, which felt as though it had been nearly completely melted off in the process. Looking it over, it was clear to him that this was almost the case.

"Dire Magistral!" a voice called out to him via the wrist-crystal. "Whatever it was that you just did, it seems to be working!" yelled Elder Mage Francis. Fighting through waves of intense pain, Grey gathered himself before speaking.

"That's good, but I don't think I can risk doing it again." he explained. "What? Why not?" asked Elder Francis, whose voice communicated that he had picked up on Grey's pain, indicated by a more sentimental and concerned tone than the militaristic one the Dire Magistral was used to hearing.

"It's too risky; I nearly lost an arm trying that out, whatever 'that' was, of course." said Grey. "Damn it. We will continue working, then!" Elder Mage Francis said finally. The Dire Magistral then rose back up shakily to his feet and looked out through a thin, slit-like window that showed a view of the skeletal ships outside, which had started picking up the pace. They were now boring down on the battleships with extreme prejudice, which was alarming to witness.

"Well, that must have really pissed you off, eh?" Grey said to himself as a slight smile began to form on his face. Granted, he was completely and utterly terrified beyond belief at the reality unfolding before him, but there was truly something great about having found out an overwhelmingly powerful enemy's weakness. It made him all the more determined to push back even harder against them. Though, of course, he didn't want to risk more of his arm or even the rest of his body to accomplish this. He was, after all, just one man.

"Dire Magistral!" cried out the voice of Elder Francis on the wrist-rock. "What is it?" Grey asked, speaking into it. "We're getting close, sir, the device is beginning to unlock!" "Very good, Francis, but I'm not sure if—huh?!" the Dire Magistral was cut off by a sudden impact that rocked the fortress around him. Taking another look outside, he could see that the skeletal ships had now caught up to them fully and were tearing apart the three ships.

His eyes alight with horror, Grey could do nothing but watch as the ribcages opened up, and humanoid shapes with glowing eyes dropped down out of them. "No!" Grey yelled as his expression became one of fury, and he quickly turned back around and rushed back over to the altar, cradling his arm as he ran. Drawing in another deep breath, and reaching outwards with shaking hands, he grabbed ahold of the weapon's handle, which sent another surge through his system as another lightning blast was sent out from the altar and vaporized the undead on the ship.

Grey let out a yell that crept up into louder decibels the longer he held onto the sword in the altar. When he found that he couldn't bear the pain anymore, the Dire Magistral tore away from the weapon and fell down once again. This time, it was more than just his arms that had been damaged, and the one he had used for the first blast had now become completely blackened and stiff. It was as if he had stuck the entirety of his upper torso in an oven. He could also feel an intense sensation of pin-pricks and needles all over. This caused him to let out a quiet, pained groan as he forced his watery eyes closed and curled back up into a fetal ball.

"Dire Magistral!" Elder Mage Francis called to him on the wrist-rock, which was on the crisped, dark arm. Grey gave no answer, finding that he didn't have any energy to speak with. "Dire Magistral!" the Elder Mage called to him once more. Summoning his strength, Grey moved his wrist over to his face and spoke into the gem. "What...is...it?" he asked in a slightly raspy tone. "We've done it! The weapon is ready!" yelled the Elder Mage in proud triumph. Grey felt a crashing wave of relief wash over him, and he found himself smiling.

"Excellent. That's great news." he replied. "We've connected it to the ship's power, should we activate it?!" asked the Elder Mage. "You have my full go-ahead. Switch it on. Burn the bastards away." ordered the Dire Magistral. A moment later, Grey could feel the battleship begin to shudder, and a slight buzz could be heard through the cold, stone floor that he was lying on. Then, a bright flash went off, flooding in through one of the windows, prompting Grey to sit up and look up in the direction it had come from. Expecting to feel an incredible, surging blast go off, Grey braced himself. But, nothing came. Instead, it was as if the flash hadn't happened in the first place.

Confused by this, Grey used the circular wall behind him to stand back up, and he hobbled over to the window where the flash of light had come from. Outside, far ahead of the ships, was a large, swirling rift that led to somewhere unknown. He couldn't make out what was on the other side of it, but it definitely appeared to be some sort of portal. "What?" he found himself asking aloud. He then lifted the wrist-rock to his mouth and asked: "Francis, what's going on?" "I don't know, sir! We thought it was a weapon of some kind, but it's..." the Elder Mage trailed off. "Francis? Francis?!" asked Grey. But, no response came. Then, he turned around and found that he wasn't alone. Standing before him, at the top of the stairs, was a rather disturbing-looking man whose eyes glowed with an umbral light.

His jaw hung loose as he drew in ragged breaths, and it was as if he weren't in full control of his facilities, seeming to sway back and forth as his arms dangled by his sides. He was dressed in Guardsmen garb, and he held a bloodied dagger in one of his hands. Grey's eyes widened with horror as the man broke into a charge towards him. Bearing the initial pain, the Dire Magistral withdrew the blade from the altar, made a quick mental prayer, and sliced horizontally, cutting away the undead with a single, swift stroke. The man's body crumbled away into ash-like powder.

He was relieved that the weapon worked, as no other weapon in the Guardsmen's history had worked on them before. This technology and the ships and weapons they had discovered and adopted was something out of the bounds of a fairy tale. He also felt a sting of remorse boil up through him over the fact that this had been one of the men he'd commanded moments prior. Shaking this off to remain focused and with his guard up, Grey then looked the weapon over once more, finding that the orange gem in its guard was giving off a faint glow, likely given to it by the altar.

"So, this is your hidden power?" Grey asked the weapon, thoroughly impressed by its capabilities. He then heard the sound of something large and otherworldly moving overhead. Throwing his eyes upwards, he could see through the square opening that there was now an enormous shape floating above the battleship. Though it was also made up of bones, it bore little resemblance to the ribcages, instead looking more like a flying saucer that had its edges fashioned into crown-like spikes.

No doubt, this was the necromancer's flagship, Grey thought. "You fool. You've placed yourself right into my hands!" Grey yelled before re-inserting the blade into the altar and sending another blast upwards. The brilliant light shot out and started to burn into the bottom of the crown ship, causing its surface to become blackened.

Grey knew that he would have to hold the weapon in place far longer this time, and he held on as long as he could. But, inevitably, he couldn't bear the pain long enough, having to tear the weapon back out of the altar's slit before the craft above could be completely destroyed. Grey yelled at the top of his lungs as he folded over, having to use the weapon as a cane to remain standing. Mustering his strength once more, the Dire Magistral looked up again and found that, though he had burned a hole straight through the crown ship, it was still mostly intact and had remained floating above the battleship.

"Damn it. Damn it!" he yelled through gritted teeth. After taking a moment to collect himself, Grey limped over to a lever on the circular wall and threw its handle upwards, causing the tower to shake ever so slightly as it started rising in a spiral-like fashion. "I'm coming for you!" Grey swore as he stared up at the crown ship with murderous vengeance in his eyes. As the bottom of the craft came closer to the tower's top, Grey braced himself once more, and a moment later, it crashed straight into the ship, bridging them.

Then, the Dire Magistral, with whatever strength he had left in him, pulled himself up a ladder that led up through the square opening. Inside the crown ship, Grey was met with pitch darkness and the dizzying stench of ancient death. Though he could not see much with it, the light of the sword's charged-up gem faintly illuminated his surroundings with an amber glow.

Taking a few cautious steps forward with his weapon raised in a defensive fashion, Grey could feel the floor give way slightly as it made a squelching sound that made him lose the contents of his stomach, which poured out onto the floor of the ship. The halls around him appeared to twist and contort, as though they were alive. Fighting through waves of nausea, Grey brought the wrist-rock up to his face and spoke into it.

"Is anyone out there? This is Dire Magistral Grey Phaselight." No response came. "Is anyone there?!" he cried. "This is Dire Magistral Grey Phaselight!" But, again, there was no response. Either the signal couldn't get through, or everyone under his command was already dead. *Or worse.* "Damn it!" Grey swore under his breath. As he continued moving through the shifting halls, which he found were made up of blackened bones held together by decaying sinew, the Dire Magistral eventually arrived at a set of gargantuan double doors that were also made of the sickening substances. Where the necromancer got stock of this sort, Grey did not want to know.

As he approached the doors, he could see that one was slightly pushed open. Sidling up alongside the closed one, he peered in and found that he could see nothing due to the other door's angle. Instinctively, he moved over to the one that was ajar and leaned against it, trying to get a better look. With horror, he realized much too late that he had put entirely too much of his weight against it, causing it to open the rest of the way and he stumbled into the room.

Grey froze. Before him was a collection of glowing eyes, and in the dank darkness he could make out dozens of silhouetted humanoid shapes that swayed much in the same way as the man from earlier. Adrenaline-filled, ice-cold blood rushed repeatedly against his eardrums. "Oh, sh—" he started to curse as the undead rushed him, overtaking him within seconds. He hadn't even had time to swing the weapon this time, finding that it had been removed from him almost instantly.

"BRING HIM TO ME." a thunderous, umbral voice boomed out from the far end of the room. Pulsing fear came over Grey as he was taken up by the crowd and brought towards the voice. He was then thrown down before someone who appeared to be sitting in some sort of throne, at least, that's what Grey's imagination told him. A pair of gleaming teal lights stared down at him, and from what could be determined in the dark, the being in the chair had long, unkempt locks of hair that went past their feet. Grey was paralyzed with palpable fear as he began to weigh his fate. In his mind, he could see flaming runes that appeared to spell out something umbral, and he heard a name being repeatedly whispered to him by what sounded like a choir of dark voices:

Ahz-Mund.....

Ahz-Mund.....

Ahz-Mund.....

The voices grew louder and stronger in a rhythmic fashion, causing him to become even dizzier than before.

AHZ-MUND.....

AHZ-MUND.....

AHZ-MUND.....

Then, a hand with an icy grasp touched his head with five fingers, and the being that sat in front of Grey spoke once more: "BE NOT AFRAID. ALL OF YOUR SUFFERING WILL BE OVER SOON." Grey was stunned by this. The owner of the voice then turned to look at the undead, and it spoke to them as well, saying: "DO NOT SUBMERGE HIM FULLY IN THE SHADOW. WE HAVE OTHER PLANS FOR THIS ONE..." commanded Ahz-Mund. With this, the undead took hold of Grey once more, and began to spew their darkness into his forced-open mouth like a fountain. For the Dire Magistral, everything started to go black and cold. As rotting fingers held his eyelids open, Grey Phaselight prayed in his mind for anything that would hear him to deliver him and his people to safety with a desperate plea. But, he was cold and alone in an uncaring world.....

Then, something feral and bestial awoke within Grey, and he felt compelled to do the necromancer's bidding for the rest of eternity as his mind became honeyed as his body began to die.....

. . .

"They've nearly breached the bridge!" yelled one of the Tech Mages, who wore a terrified expression on his young face. "What are we going to do? Phaselight is gone!" yelled another. Elder Mage Francis wracked his aged brain for the right answer, but any and all ideas that came to him were full of holes and involved far too much risk. The mantle of leadership had fallen to him, as the other Guardsmen had left the bridge in order to defend the upper and lower decks from the invading undead.

Of all the men that could have been tasked with this heavy burden, the Elder Mage felt as though he were completely ill-equipped to handle it. Looking out through the thick glass view screen that spanned nearly the entirety of the stone ship's square bridge, the old man could see that the other two vehicles had fallen to a similar fate, as what looked like a sea of undead humanoids and other creatures covered almost all of its exterior.

Damn. Francis thought to himself. Then, an idea dawned upon him, and he went with it. "Whatever lies on the other side of that rift can't possibly be worse than what we're already dealing with. The ship is lost, let's move! We need to make it to one of the escape crafts. Scion Callow," he paused, indicating one of the younger Tech-Mages in the room, "Get the assets aboard a transport. Ensign Lewis, you'll be up front with me!" Elder Francis commanded and unplugged the alien cube from the ship's power socket and kept it close to his chest.

He then led the way into the elevator and brought the last of those who were on the bridge of the doomed ship with him down into the hangar bay, being sure to stop at the storage room to let Psion Callow out. "I'll be down with them soon, don't wait for me!" Callow said as he ran out of the elevator, which closed back up behind him and it began to lower once more.. When the doors of the elevator re-opened, they were met with the sights of pure, unadulterated chaos.

The Guardsmen and Tech-Mages that were equipped to fight were struggling against the undead, who vastly outnumbered them and clearly had the upper hand. "Move, now! Let's get aboard one of those!" commanded Elder Mage Francis, who then led the group into one of the nearby dropships, which resembled a small bunker with rotating thrusters on it. Just as they were all about to make it, some of the undead took notice of this and snatched away two of the Tech-Mages, who screamed as they were taken and turned by their zombified comrades. Once the remaining survivors were all packed in, Francis keyed in the buttons necessary to close the door to the vehicle, closing them into the small space.

Francis and the ensign took their seats at the front of the vehicle while the others strapped into the chairs lining the rest of the craft's cramped interior. The Elder Mage worked quickly to plug in the alien box while the ensign started the small ship's engines. "Hold onto something!" hollered the ensign, who raised the vehicle up into the air before activating the thrusters and sending them rocketing forward at a break-neck pace out of the magick-shielded doorway of the docking bay.

"Sir, where are we even going?!" asked one of the younger Tech-Mages. "In there!" replied Francis as he pointed out towards the rift. Though they were uncertain if this was a smart (or even safe) move, the other Tech-Mages trusted in their superior. "What will the others do?!" cried another Tech-Mage. "They're a lost cause, we can't risk going back there!" answered Elder Francis.

This was far from a reassuring answer, but the others had to agree with his logic. The necromancer's forces were at their backs; there really was nothing more they could have done, given the circumstances. Still, the loss of life was too terrible to bear, causing a few of the Tech-Mages to begin weeping as they mourned the loss of their friends and comrades.

"We're pulling in now!" exclaimed the ensign as the dropship approached the rift. It was then that something landed on top of them, indicated by a loud *THUD!* and the craft being jostled about for a moment. "Oh no!" cried Elder Francis. The identity of what had dropped on them was soon revealed in the form of several undead crawling to the front of the craft and looking down from its roof and in through the windshield at their potential victims.

"Not good, not good!" yelled Francis, who then ordered the ensign: "Shake them loose!" The ensign followed the order, performing a few hard veers left and right and a barrel-roll that shook most of them loose. Some still remained, and the haunting glow of their vacant eyes was terrifying as they stared at the survivors. "Sir, I can't shake all of them!" cried the ensign. "Never mind that, pull us through, now!" ordered Francis, and the ensign guided the vehicle through the glowing rift.

Once they were on the other side, they could tell immediately that the space around the craft was vastly different to the one found in their dimension, being void of the black mist and appearing to be far more empty than the bounds of their world, perplexing and intriguing all of them. "What is this place?" asked the ensign. Elder Mage Francis stared out in awe of the discovery. "I'm not fully certain, but...I think this may be another realm entirely..." he explained.

The Elder Mage was completely taken by what he was witnessing. "What? How?!" asked one of the other Tech-Mages. "I don't know, but we'd better close the rift before—" Francis was cut off by the appearance of a looming shadow that passed over the small craft. "Oh no, they've followed us through! Quickly, close it! Close the rift!" cried one of the Tech-Mages. Ignoring the momentary insubordination, Elder Mage Francis worked quickly to try and key in a reverse of the sequence that had opened it earlier.

Looking through the rearview feed on the ensign's dashboard, the Elder Mage could see that the rift had closed up. But, not before a handful of the ribcages got through. "Damn!" the Elder Mage cursed. "Open another rift, we might lose them that way!" cried one of the younger Tech-Mages.

"No way! Are you crazy?! What if it reopens the same one, and the Unwilling flood in?!" cried another. Weighing the possibilities, the Elder Mage decided it was for the best to give it another try. "Ensign, take us away from here—" The escape craft was stopped dead in its tracks by one of the ribcages grabbing ahold of the vehicle. The Tech-Mages shrieked in terror as they realized what had happened. Then, they were pulled backwards by the giant skeletal limb.

"Quickly, into the escape pods!" ordered the Elder Mage, and the others quickly heeded this command. "How are we going to get away?! One of the Tech-Mages asked Francis, who pondered this for but a moment. "We'll use it, but not all of us will be able to make it this time." he said as calmly as he could, given the situation. He was suddenly very sullen as the realization of what must be done connected in his head.

"I'll be a decoy. The rest of you need to get out of here!" he yelled. In a frantic panic, they each took one of the pods, which were like large, windowed stone test tubes with a single thruster at their backs. He then handed over the alien device to the ensign and walked him through activating it. "Hook it up to the pod's energy source, key in this sequence, then push *this*. It performs an impossible calculation, to my own estimations. Then, reverse the order to close the rift behind you." The Elder Mage demonstrated the sequence to the ensign and then indicated a particular runic button on the side of the device.

The ensign looked terribly unsure of whether this would work or not, but they had little choice otherwise. "It was an honor, sir." he said tearfully. "No, son, the honor was mine. Now, go!" barked the Elder Mage, who then boarded his pod and keyed in a button that caused the door to it to close up behind him.

It then shot out of the dropship like a torpedo, and the others followed suit quickly after. The pods fired out and dispersed into the space around the dropship in several directions. Then, most of them grouped up into a single direction, following the one the ensign was in. A moment later, a second rift was opened. The pod that housed the Elder Mage suddenly rocketed around in the opposite direction as Francis tried to desperately pull the attention of the Unwilling away from his comrades.

This utterly failed, as the ribcage ships started to close in on the escape pods. "No...no!" cried Francis, who thumped the bottom of his fist against the window of the pod in frustration. There then came a small sense of relief as he witnessed the ensign's pod make it through the rift with a handful of others before it closed, trapping him and the remaining few behind. They were at the mercy of the Unwilling, who were soon upon them.

Elder Mage Francis made his peace with his fate as he began to quietly recite a prayer mantra to himself. Suddenly, dozens of rifts opened up around him and the Unwilling spilled out through them. Elder Mage Francis' eyes became wide with horror as he realized the grave error they had made. *There was more than one of the devices onboard the Artoum.* Soon enough, he would lose all sense of freedom and become enslaved to the will of the necromancer...

With their newfound capability, Ahz-Mund's Unwilling began to pour into every known realm in existence, setting off the largest scale invasion in the history of the multiverse. Unchecked and unstoppable, not a single world was safe from his grasp.....

Running in fear will only prolong the inevitable....

THE ENEMY FROM BEYOND

Stage I:

The Maiden Voyage

(Across worlds, and some years later...)

As he cut the thin pieces of rusted sheet

metal away from the derelict's outer hull with his

plasma torch, the sweat that was accumulating on

Sonder's forehead began to trickle down into his

indigo-colored eyes, drawing his ire. Ear-length

locks of frost-white hair stuck to the sides of his

young face. If it hadn't been for the fact that he

was wearing a vacuum-sealed helmet, he could

have taken care of this annoyance rather easily.

The electronic fans inside his suit rig had

died after his first week on the job, which was to

be expected when working for a cost-cutting space-faring conglomerate like *Mistral*, whose resources were spread thin as it is. Newer and working equipment was for top performers and special cases. Sonder, sadly, was neither of these things. Though, this was due more to circumstance than anything else.

Reflecting on this for a moment while he continued cutting, the young man realized that he had been working himself to the bone for the better part of three whole years. He exhaled a short huff of breath at this and shook his head slightly. The question that had been nagging him for most of his time with the company came back to the forefront of his mind once again: *what am I doing here?* Knowing that it was for the better to shrug it off and keep working, Sonder did his best to focus on the job at hand.

As he lifted away the panel of metal, he hummed along to the song that was coming from his suit's internal radio system. Though the cassette's quality was crunchy and warbled from how worn out it was, it sure beat the silence of space.

Just when the best part of the song was ramping up, the cassette stopped, prompting Sonder to shut his eyes, lean his head back, and groan. The sound was lost to the great, silent abyss around him. "Really? Now? I thought I just changed the batteries on this stupid thing..." Sonder said aloud to himself, his voice muffled by the spacesuit's helmet.

Out in the pitch-black vacuum, without anything to distract him now, Sonder felt a sense of dread start to overtake him as the silence crept in. After taking a deep breath of recycled air, he re-centered his focus on cutting away more of the scuttled ship's sheet metal as fast as he could. Nothing unsettled Sonder more than the quiet of the endless void around him. It was times like these that made him question why he even took a job like this in the first place. But then again, he had little choice in what career he could go with. In a world such as the one he found himself living in, this really was the best that he could get. At least, for the time being (he hoped).

There then came a great shadow over Sonder, one that made his blood run cold as he quickly turned to confirm his worst fears; the rugged and rusted vehicle was one of *corsair* designation, indicated by the crudely painted-on death's head that adorned one of its sides. How these savage men eluded imprisonment was beyond Sonder, as was his ability to fight them off.

It was then that a bolt of plasma seared into the derelict's hull to Sonder's left. It had missed him by a decent degree, cluing him in to the fact that they weren't out for his blood—just his salvage. If they wanted him dead, they would have done him in when they had a greater chance to moments earlier. Still, Sonder wasn't taking any chances, and he scrambled up the ladder of the metal panel (cursing fervently to himself as he went) and climbed quickly over its top, taking shelter inside a large, blown-out opening in the derelict's hull (likely caused by whatever space skirmish that had sunk it).

On his way inside, Sonder bumped his head against the side of the spacesuit's helmet, causing him to vividly recall something he had long forgotten.

. . .

As he gently drifted about in the cold, dark of space with a depleting supply of air, he could do nothing as someone floated over to him. Though he did not recognize their identity, something in his mind clued him into knowing that this was a friendly face that had been with him for some time. They unplugged and removed the breathing apparatus from their suit and plugged it into his, replacing the damaged one. Within moments, he had air again. The last thing he saw was their face through a one-way glass visor mouthing the words: "Spend it wisely." (in reference to the last bit of air they had) and smiling sorrowfully before kicking off from him and launching into the void, never to be seen again. As they did this, Sonder reached out much like a child for their parent, but he was powerless to save them...

. . .

Sonder could feel the impact of about a dozen or so more bolts sear into the panel behind him as he curled up against its curved frame, snapping him back to reality. His head was throbbing. After this all had ceased, Sonder gave it a good moment or two before mustering the courage he needed in order to climb back up and take a peek. Once he had done so, he could do nothing but watch as the corsair ship grabbed ahold of his work pod with an enormous metal claw (typically reserved for gathering scrab) and cracked it open like a nut, causing a small explosion as a result that sent shrapnel from the new wreckage in every direction.

Through the silence, Sonder could have sworn that he heard the men cackling inside their ship as it took off with the net filled with his hard work and disappeared into the endless night of space. *Great*. Sonder thought to himself as his mood completely died in that instant. He also wondered where that daydream had come from.

Knowing that groaning would only prolong his being saved, Sonder keyed in the sequence of inputs on his suit's wrist-worn device that sent out an S.O.S. signal to Mistral HQ. If he was lucky, it would only take them a few hours to retrieve him.

Unfortunately, he knew that reality wouldn't be that kind to him, and by the end of an entire day later, a second work pod arrived, this one being automated by a Protocol Intelligence. After climbing inside and allowing everything to pressurize, Sonder removed his helmet, allowing his pale skin to breathe, and for him to finally wipe the sweat from his forehead. "Well, I'm really in for it this time..." he said aloud to himself as he shook his head before relaxing into the worn padding of the pilot's chair. At the very least, Sonder was grateful for the fact that the Protocol

Intelligence would be the one driving this time, giving him ample time to rest up.

. . .

"You're fired!" shouted Sonder's boss. The words tore straight through Sonder. His indigo-colored eyes widened from shock, and an uneasy sensation filled his core. "What?" he found himself asking aloud, and his clean-shaven, porcelain-featured face took on a startled and confused expression. Sonder's shoulders tightened, then sagged as the reality of what was happening started to set in. "Wh-why, though?" Sonder asked his boss with a puzzled tone.

"Because you haven't met the quota a single time this entire season, boy!" yelled the portly, middle-aged man. "But—" Sonder started to say, but he was cut off by his boss. "No 'buts!' You had a job to do, and that was to bring back an agreed-upon amount of scrap and junk, and your numbers were nowhere near where they should be! You think I'm just gonna let you keep doing that for another few months? No sir!" Sonder's boss shook his head as he stood up from his desk chair and started to move towards the office door.

Grabbing ahold of its handle, Sonder's boss practically tore it open and motioned with a firm, straightened-out hand for him to leave. For a moment, silence filled the room, and both men were still. "But, what about my insurance? How am I supposed to—?" Sonder was interrupted once again by his boss. "Don't know, don't care. Go!" Sonder, who had still been seated, hung his head as he rose up slowly and turned towards the exit.

"And...what about the medications that I still need filling...?" Sonder tried to explain, but his words fell on deaf ears. In fact, his boss let loose a chuckle at this. "So what? You and everybody else, pal. That privilege belongs to hard-working folk, not street trash like you." Sonder's boss said in a gruff, uncaring tone.

At this, the young man felt his entire body go practically numb as he shuffled slowly and shakily towards the door. "Now get out, would ya?! Sheesh, it's gonna be hell trying to find your replacement. Sooner I get workin' on that, the better." Sonder's boss said finally as he closed the door right behind him before muttering curses under his breath and throwing his arms about. As it shut into place, it bumped Sonder forward slightly, knocking him into the rest of his life.

With that, Sonder's entire world had come crumbling down. He weighed the option of submitting a plea to the Employee Resources office, but he knew that this would be in vain, for he was small fry in a world filled to the brim with problems, and that line was already immeasurably long. His joints and back ached deeply, and the small cuts on his hands pulsed with pain.

After ambling like a zombie past thousands of cubicles and riding the stuffy, cramped elevator down to the lobby, Sonder walked in a hollow manner towards the sliding front entrance doors and stepped out into the cold of the outside world. The frigid air interacting with the sweat stains on his jumpsuit made him feel as though he were freezing, adding to his misery.

Without looking back at the enormous building (which was adorned with a large, burned-out 'M' for Mistral, the very same logo that was on the breast pocket and shoulder of Sonder's uniform), Sonder started to amble towards the train stop, following the faded, color-coded neon line on the concrete ground towards his destination. The cloud-smothered sun in the sky felt like a distant, unreachable light, and the smoggy air of the dreary industrial zone did little to offer Sonder any sense of refreshment.

There wasn't a tree, nor grass field, nor blooming flower in sight. The natural world of the planet had been consumed and suppressed in an effort to totally industrialize the surface of Sonder's home world. Tall smokestacks gushed forth huge plumes of multi-colored excess smoke in the back of District 37.

Sonder's mind shifted back-and-forth between being overloaded with questions and blocking all of these out at a feverish rate. Either way, he was completely miserable, and it was as if his sense of direction had completely fallen apart before his very eyes. Though he knew he had been wronged, as he had truly done his best to meet the unrealistic expectations of the company he had exhausted himself for and had his scored cheated out from under him by corsairs, Sonder had taken his position in life for granted.

Putting together a back-up plan felt pointless in the world he found himself living in. Pursuing something scholarly would bury him in a lifetime's worth of debt, and he had tried every other career door that was available to him to no avail. As he boarded and took his seat inside the magnetic train car that had just arrived, Sonder's thoughts shifted to swirling questions regarding his parents' whereabouts.

A profound headache came over him as the usual amnesia set in. Everything had been a mess since he could remember. It frustrated Sonder to no end to know that he might never have his answers. Still, his mind asked painful question after question, bombarding his bruised temporal lobe to a point of nausea. He forced his eyes shut and brought his hands up to the sides of his head, massaging them in an attempt to soothe the splitting headache that had overtaken him.

When the pangs started to subside, Sonder moved his hands away and found that he could open his eyes again. He then witnessed a fluffy, pitch-black shape rush past, startling him. Instinctively reacting to this, he pulled his legs up and tightened them to his body and turned slightly in a protective manner as he let out a yelp-like sound. Sonder then watched as dozens more of the fluffy shapes ran across the floor of the train.

They appeared to be some sort of wolf-like creatures with long fangs and a glowing patterning that ran throughout their bodies like a bolt of lightning. The wolves were gently snatching up some of the train passengers' belongings before bolting off towards the next car over.

"What the—?" Sonder asked aloud to no one in particular. He was completely flabbergasted. For a moment, he began to wonder if he had passed out on the train and was dreaming. As active as his imagination could be, this was no dream. When the wolves had gone, Sonder and the other passengers of the train were left to their own, very confused devices.

He then took notice of something moving around outside the train's window. Something puzzled him about what he was seeing, prompting him to rub his eyes and squint. It looked to him as though some sort of aircraft were pulling up alongside the train and inching ever slightly more close to it. It was unlike any sort of flying craft he had seen. Flecks of rust dotted its greyish body, and its silhouette was akin to a gigantic bird of prey. Once it was close enough, the vehicle lifted up higher and disappeared from view as it went over the train.

Sonder could have sworn that he heard what sounded to him like loud hard rock music accompanying the craft, likely coming from inside it. He then turned around and looked out the window behind him to see if it would show up there, but it hadn't. Instead, he could hear the music coming from overhead now. A moment later, it sounded like something—no, a few somethings—landed on top of the car.

Then came a rhythmic series of thumps that became quieter as they receded from where he was sitting. There was no doubt in Sonder's mind at this point: *they were about to be robbed by corsairs*. A bubble of hot anger started to accumulate in his core, and he took on a scowl as his heart rate began to accelerate. This time, he wouldn't let them get away with it.

As he rose up onto his sore feet, the stranger sitting next to him grabbed ahold of his arm, startling Sonder, who then looked over at the worn, tired, and weary face of a worried old man. The man gave a slow, disapproving shake of his head, seeming to hopefully discourage Sonder from confronting the corsairs. The young man's shoulders sagged, and the fire inside of him quieted down. But then, the urge to chase after them came over him once more, and the fire was reignited.

Sonder tore away from the old man's grip and broke into a bolting run, following the sound of the receding footsteps. Rushing past countless other patrons (who were just as startled by these events as he was) and bounding through the slid-open doorways that connected the cars to one another, Sonder soon caught up to the sounds above and witnessed the top hatch of the car he found himself in being forcibly broken open.

A thick rope unrolled as it entered the opening, and what Sonder presumed to be a corsair lowered themselves down it and into the train. He locked eyes with the man—a young, muscle-y fellow of around his age who was dressed in black jeans, a dark grey tank top, and combat boots— who towered above him. A black jacket was tied around his waist. The corsair had long, rusty-red hair that was partly tied up into a bun and looked as though he hadn't shaved his face for a few days. He had grey eyes that communicated a sense of humanity that Sonder hadn't expected to see in a corsair. Though, they were still fraught with worry.

Usually, corsairs bore a madman-like demeanor, from Sonder's own recollection of personal encounters. But with this one, there was, to his own estimations, no sense of ill-will or malice about him, something that made Sonder question a great deal about the situation in the moment.

The man took on a surprised expression as he stared at Sonder before he turned and broke into a run in the direction of the car ahead without uttering a word or noise. "Wait, stop!" yelled Sonder, hoping that his words would be enough. But, he knew better. The man continued running and made his way into the next train car, prompting Sonder to follow after him at a quickened pace. Onlookers watched with eyes alight with horror and bated breath as they witnessed the chase.

As he ran under the rope that led up to the train's roof, Sonder looked up and froze in place as a large, blue-plated and red strip-light-lit mechanical being dropped down onto him, causing him to fall to the floor and get pinned by its heavy frame as the wind was knocked out from him.

Sonder was almost certain he had cracked a few ribs in the process, and yet all the synthform had to offer him was a simple "Apologies." as it looked down at him with its mechanical head (which resembled a boxy camera with multiple lenses) before launching off of him and into a rhythmic run, following the path of the rusty-red-haired man.

Pain surged through Sonder, who groaned loudly as he withdrew into a fetal-like position in an attempt to comfort himself. The world around him became blurry, and the last thing he saw as he looked around with his consciousness fading were the shapes of the two corsairs bounding through the train cars at a quick pace and the fluffy shapes of the wolf-like creatures closing in around him.

Their glowing red eyes were strangely alluring to him. Then, everything went dark.

. . .

When Sonder awoke, he found that a slight ache had replaced the pulsing pain from earlier and that he was somewhere he did not recognize. He was lying down on a flat, rectangular padded table and around him was the interior of what looked like a very small rendition of a medical wing. Above him was a series of fluorescent lightbulbs that flickered slightly. The air around him tasted stale, as if it had been recycled countless times through a dated filtration system in dire need of a good cleaning.

He could hear a mechanical chugging through the walls that vibrated the entire room around him ever so slightly. His brown jumpsuit uniform had been removed, as was the shirt he had on underneath it, leaving him solely in his underwear. A strange, white pad was taped over his chest.

It was then that the recent memory of his encounter with the corsairs came rushing back to him and panic began to overtake him. However, as he tried sitting up, he realized that he had been strapped to the table he was laying on. Overcome with immense fear, Sonder began to writhe and push against the straps with the vain hope that he would be able to loosen or break them.

When this failed, his mind began to race as he considered the possibility that he was about to be probed, have his organs harvested to be sold on the black market, or that he was about to be an unwilling victim of some horrific, off-the-records experimental medical procedure. It didn't help that his strength hadn't fully returned, adding further to the stress of his situation.

Just as he was about to start breaking down and screaming for help (which was really about the only thing he could do), Sonder could hear the muffled sounds of a somewhat heated conversation coming from outside the room he was in. This grew louder as the pair who were having it drew closer to the door. Looking up from the table in the direction of the chatter, Sonder watched with bated breath as the metal, windowed door slid automatically open with a squeal, revealing two individuals that he assumed to be corsairs who then stepped inside the room.

One he recognized—the rusty-red-haired and burly man—while the other was a slender and boyish-looking fellow who was about half the man's height. He had a pair of thick, black rectangular glasses, platinum-blonde hair with blue highlights that had grown down past his ears, and wore an oversized grey, hooded jacket with very long sleeves, baggy pants, and worn-down high-top sneakers.

"—not my fault he got in the way." said the man that Sonder recognized. He had some kind of electronic smoke pen in his hand that he took a drag off of after saying this. The man then exhaled an impressively large plume of white vapor into the room that smelled of cinnamon. "Do you really have to do that in here?" the other corsair asked in a fair, higher-pitched tone, sounding concerned. "What? It helps me relax." the redhead bit back. "It's awful for your health, though..." "Why do you care? What's it to you?" "Never mind, whatever."

When the pair noticed that Sonder was awake on the table, their demeanor shifted immediately from argumentative to apprehensive and careful. The boy that Sonder hadn't recognized walked cautiously over to him and had a sympathetic, nervous expression on his lightly-freckled and delicately-featured face. His glimmering, emerald-green eyes were fraught with worry. Though Sonder didn't exactly have a thing for other guys, there was something pretty about him.

"Hey, guy, you feeling okay?" he asked Sonder earnestly. Sonder was stunned. Normally, corsairs weren't exactly the talk-y type, something that threw him off. Instead, he sounded gentle and sincere. "Do you have any residual pain?" the boy continued with his questioning. Sonder let out a groan as he pressed lightly into his chest. "Oh man, *Ayb* really did a number on you back there. I'd scold him again, but that would be lost on him. That old *synthform* has very little regard for the safety of soft and squishy *mortalforms* like you and me. It's kinda why we keep him around though; he's damn good in a fight." The young corsair explained.

At this, Sonder summoned the strength he needed in order to speak. "Who are you people? Where am I?" he asked the bespectacled boy. The corsair pulled back from Sonder and his face took on a more conflicted appearance as he seemed to weigh something in his mind. "Well," he started to say as he looked over at the other man in the room for help.

"Don't look at me, it was your idea to bring him on board, *Jasper*." answered the rusty-red-haired man, who had an annoyed expression on his face. "What were we supposed to do? The *Captain* is—" "The Captain is predisposed at the moment." the other cut him off. "I know that, but you're the one who gave the orders in his place back there. This is completely your fault, *Klay*. If the Captain wasn't...well, *you know*, we probably wouldn't be in this situation to begin with." Jasper countered.

"Alright, alright, ease off on me, would ya? This hasn't exactly been a good day for any of us. I mean, just look at him." said Klay, who gestured to Sonder on the table. "Uh, guys? Can you let me up, please?" the white-haired worker asked the pair of corsairs in an anxious, polite tone. The last thing he wanted to do was cause any possible upset, as he was still completely at their mercy. Of course, had they intended any harm, they would have likely done him in already by then. "Sure, but we gotta ask first; *you're not going to retaliate for what happened back there, are you?*" Klay asked him, looking severe as he stepped closer.

Sonder looked confused at this. "Uh, no? Why would I?" he asked in reply. At this, Jasper and Klay exchanged a look between each other and then returned their focus to Sonder. After seeming to brace themselves, they undid the belts on the table, allowing him to sit up and move around freely. "Take it slow and easy, your body is still recovering from *the procedure*." cautioned Jasper. "Procedure?" Sonder asked, becoming increasingly worried after hearing this. He rubbed his chest and sides, and his core was sore all over from having what felt like a couple tons of walking machinery drop down onto him. It was clear that his ribs had been broken from this, but it now felt as if he were several weeks into recovery.

"Don't worry, it was nothing invasive. It's just, well, all of your ribs were completely shattered by Ayb." explained Jasper. "But, thanks to some impressive pieces of medical equipment we borrowed, you're almost as good as new." he added. "Stole." Klay corrected him. "*Borrowed*." Jasper insisted as he shot Klay a look. "Still, I'd advise you to be careful; you're not fully healed just yet. It's going to take a few days for you to fully recover." he added.

"Um, thank you." said Sonder. Klay and Jasper were thrown off by this, as if they expected him to blow up on them or be rendered completely mute by this disturbing chain of events. "Oh, uh, you're welcome, guy." said Jasper, who rubbed the back of his neck nervously and gave a faint smile.

"So, what's your name?" he then asked. Sonder thought this over for a moment, wondering if he should divulge this sort of information to the corsairs. Ultimately, he decided that it couldn't hurt if they knew. "Sonder." he said simply. "Sonder...?" Jasper asked and gestured with his hand, hoping to get a last name as well. "That's my name; Sonder." the white-haired worker answered. "You don't have a family name?" Klay asked him. Sonder shook his head.

"Hmm. That's kinda weird, man." commented Klay. "I'm Jasper Kasperian, jack-of-all-trades. I do just about everything that Klay and the others don't. It's nice to meet you, Sonder. Though, I wish it were under better circumstances. This here is—"

"Klayborne; I'm the ship's gunner and mechanic." the rusty-red-haired man interrupted in a gruff manner and then cleared his throat before walking over to Sonder and extending his hand outwards. Sonder returned this gesture and shook his hand somewhat loosely, primarily due to low energy and nerves that refused to settle. He could feel that Klay's was somewhat reserved, as if there was trust to be earned.

"I go by my last name. It's just a personal preference, don't think too hard about it, 'kay?" explained Klay. Jasper smirked and snickered quietly over this. "Um, okay. So, where exactly am I?" Sonder asked, reiterating his second question from earlier. "You're aboard our ship. This is our little medical room." explained Jasper, who gestured around the room with his arms spread out.

At this, a tidal wave of reality came crashing down onto Sonder, and he suddenly became increasingly worked-up. His eyes widened and he began to sweat profusely. "Wait, I'm on your ship? But, I have to get home, I have to—" Sonder was becoming frantic. "Whoa, whoa, just calm down." said Jasper in a soothing tone as he held his hands up in a peace-offering gesture.

"No, you don't understand, I've just been fired from my job, I have so much I need to sort out. My insurance, my medical coverage, my living situation—" "I understand, but you really should calm down—" "No, you don't understand!

Take me back, right now!" Sonder's voice had crept up into a yell.

"Out of the question." said Klay, who sounded firm and unmovable. Sonder looked over at him with a shocked expression on his face. "Why's that?" he asked him. Jasper looked suddenly very guilty. "Let's just say there's really no point in going back there." Klay explained. "So, you're holding me against my will?" Sonder asked, his indigo eyes still widened. "No, not exactly. It's just that, well...your home world *probably* doesn't exist anymore."

Sonder was dumbfounded. "What do you mean by that?" he asked Klay, who didn't exactly look thrilled to be saying something like that. "Klay, we don't know that for—" "I think we do, Jas'. You've seen the map, right? Pretty sure *they've* consumed it already." said Klay, sounding defeated. "Wait, what? What's going on? What are you talking about?" asked Sonder. "He'd probably think we're just crazy if we told him." Klay said to Jasper.

"Well, then why don't we *show* him? It's the least we can do, right?" Jasper offered in reply. Klay mulled this over for a moment before meeting Jasper's eyes once more and said: "Maybe." Jasper then turned to Sonder with a somewhat eager expression. "It'll be okay, Klay. I mean, hey, we were all uninitiated at some point or another." "Yeah, and our minds broke, didn't they?" "Well, that's..." Jasper trailed off and rubbed the back of his neck again.

It was then that the automatic door slid open once again, revealing a young woman dressed in a brown flight jacket and cargo pants. She had flowing, wavy golden hair, and her eyes were the color of the deep ocean. "Oh, I'm sorry!" she exclaimed as she covered her face with her hands and then peeked through them as she began to blush. Jasper and Klay looked at Sonder and made the realization as well. "Let's, uh, get you dressed, pal." said Klay, who sounded very uncomfortable. Jasper snorted and laughed at this, the sound joyous and soft.

. . .

Once he had finished dressing in the cramped bathroom, which had all of the trappings one might find in such a place (only it all looked suited for air and space travel), Sonder filled the sink basin and splashed his face with water. Finding it to be ice-cold, he couldn't help but mutter a few curses under his breath in surprise. He then dried his face with the provided towel and then turned and pressed the button on the panel next to the windowless door, which slid open to reveal Klay, Jasper, and the girl leaning against the railing that hung from the beige walls.

"You know, I'm kind of sad it's another one of you boys. I was hoping he'd be a girl. It gets so lonely up here by myself." The golden-haired girl said to Klay and Jasper, sounding exasperated. She then turned and walked over to Sonder. "Sorry about that, I didn't know that the boys hadn't given you your clothes back yet." she explained with a smile, sounding as though she was still finding it amusing. "It's okay." said Sonder, who was still flushed in the face.

"I'm Mason, by the way. Mason Vohldt." said the third corsair as she took Sonder's hand and shook it. The white-haired worker blushed even harder when he found that her hands were soft, warm, and delicate to the touch. The pair of deep-blue sapphires set into her face were entrancing, and Sonder could swear that she, too, was slightly red in the face. *She had a nice smile, too.* Sonder thought to himself.

"I'm the pilot and owner of this fine bird. *She's* been in my family's possession for a long time, exchanged hands through several generations. Sure wish they took better care of her before I got to have her, though." Mason continued. "Oh wow." said Sonder, finding anything she said to be truly enthralling. Really, he just liked to watch her mouth move. He hadn't ever had the chance to talk to many girls before this, at least to his recollection.

A slight pang went off in his head when he tried to look back in his memories, causing him to raise his hand up to soothe it. "Uh oh, you doing okay? I hear Ayb smashed you up good back there. Jasper tells me your recovery is going well, though." Mason asked. "Yeah, I'll be fine. It's just...it's nothing." said Sonder, waving it away. "Okay, just making sure. Would you like a brief tour? I feel like we may as well, since you'll be staying with us until we find you a new home." Mason offered. "Sure." Sonder said in reply. Klay shook his head at this, as if this was all a waste of time.

"Awesome, well come along, then." said Mason, who took Sonder by the hand and led him through the hall of her ship. On either side of the worn, tan hall were several windowed and windowless grey doors that led to various rooms. There were symbols in a language he didn't recognize painted onto them as some sort of indicator. They were likely numbers, he estimated. He began to wonder if this was an alien craft, or if it was so old that its language looked alien. Sonder was already familiar with the infirmary in the back and the bathroom he had just come out of, leaving just a handful of others to be shown off.

"That's the loading ramp room," Mason explained as she pointed to the door at the back of the hall. "This here leads to our engine room, it's where all the magic happens." Mason then said as she gestured towards the hatch on the tightly-grated metal floor. "Our personal quarters are these ones here," she then gestured to a few of the rooms on either side of the hall, "and this one is yours." she finished explaining as she led Sonder over to its door, pressed in the button on the panel next to it, and pulled him inside.

The interior was somewhat ratty, appearing to be another storage room with a couple of standing refrigerators that were bolted to the floor. "Don't worry, I'll have Klay make it up for you." she assured him with a smile. Klay sighed at this. "And then, we have the best place on the ship back this way." Mason explained as she led Sonder back out of the room and towards the black door at the end of the hall, which slid open to reveal what looked like a large, open cockpit with a handful of seats. To the left of the doorway was a curved wall with a smaller door that had a sign taped to it that read: "under maintenance." It looked as though it led to some sort of upper level of the ship.

The centermost seat, set at the far end of the bridge room, was clearly intended for the pilot, as it had various knobs, levers, and a pair of control sticks set into its armrests and sides. In front of this console was a series of small screens that were adorned with security feeds, a radar, and positional data. Beyond this was the spectacular view of the vacuum void. Tiny, glittering coins were set into the blanket of midnight, indicating that they were somewhere out in deep space.

Though, something seemed off or different about this to Sonder. He couldn't exactly put his finger on it. "Where are we?" he asked Mason without taking his eyes off of the sights. "Sector H, Quadrant...9, I believe?" she didn't sound entirely too sure of this. Sonder turned and gave her a look of concern. "Oh don't worry, we're not lost. I've just gotten used to Ayb being the navigator." she explained and gestured to the large, blue box that was nestled into a socket space next to the pilot's console. "You can come out now, Ayb. There's someone you should meet." Mason said, speaking to the box, which rolled out from its place and began to open up back into the form that Sonder had been previously acquainted with.

The azure-plated robotic being rose to its full height and walked over to Sonder and Mason with heavy, mechanical steps that shook the room slightly as it moved. Once it was close enough,

Sonder could make out a serial designation in white stenciling that was worn away slightly on its breastplate that read: *TLMCS-AYB.* "Now, remember your manners, Ayb. This is Sonder. He's the most recent victim of your war path." Mason said to it. There was something unsettling about how still the robot had become. Its bulky frame, red strip-lighting, and camera-like head were cold and intimidating in the low-lit grey room.

"Hello." it said to Sonder in a deep growl of a robotic tone. Its tinny voice sounded as though it were coming through a radio speaker. "Uh, hi." Sonder said back to it. "Ayb, what do we say to those we've trampled ?" "Move?" it turned on its servos and asked Mason. "No! Apologize to him, dummy." she corrected the droid, who then turned back to face Sonder. "My bad." it said simply, and in a flat tone. Finding that it really couldn't be helped, Sonder returned this with a simple: "It's all good." Though, he didn't sound entirely too sure if this had been an adequate enough apology.

"Next time, watch where you're going, eh?" Mason said to Ayb and punched one of his metal arms in a friendly, encouraging manner. Sonder's eyes widened at this, thinking she was going to set it off and get them all killed. He then relaxed when he saw that the robotic being hadn't reacted to this. "Now that you've met our resident murder-droid, why don't you take a seat? Here, get comfortable. Pick any one you want." Mason offered. "Not that one!" hollered Klay, who had entered the bridge with Jasper in tow, indicating the seat that Sonder was about to choose.

"That's my spot." Klay explained as he got closer. "Excuse *you*, it's my ship, he can sit wherever he'd like." Mason said defiantly and gave Klay a scolding look before returning to Sonder and giving him a friendly smile. The white-haired worker chose the seat opposite of that, which was next to the pilot's, and nestled into it. Though it was sunken-in from use, it was plush and warm. "Comfy, yeah?" Mason asked him. Sonder nodded and eased back all the way into it, breathing a quiet sigh as he did so. Mason let out a giggle at this.

"Forgive me, it's just, it's been so long since we've had anyone join our crew. It's kind of refreshing to have a new face around." she explained. "Can I show you somethin' cool?" she then offered as she sat down in the pilot's chair. "Sure." said Sonder, whose curiosity had been piqued. At this, Mason turned a few of the dials on her control console and flicked on some switches. An audible buzz filled the room. "Here...we...go." she said as she flicked a few more switches.

Suddenly, the rich sound of rock music boomed out into the air, startling Sonder, and causing him to cover his ears. No 'ifs,' 'ands,' or 'buts' about it, this was most definitely the ship he had seen earlier that day. Sonder could feel the bass of the beat resounding in his bones. To his left, Mason bobbed her head to the song as a wide grin cut across her face. The entire ship seemed to shake with the sound.

"Sounds great, right?!" Mason asked, having to shout over it for Sonder to hear her. "What?!" he asked with blown-out ear drums. "I said: sounds great, doesn't it?!" she asked again. Sonder gave a weary expression and a thumbs-up in reply, causing her to laugh, which was barely audible over the crashing blasts. After a moment, she turned one of the dials down, and the volume receded to a much more acceptable decibel.

"I just had this bad boy installed about a month ago." she explained to Sonder. "Did you steal it?" he asked. Mason looked at him with a slight twinge of guilt in her facial expression. "Maaaaybe." she answered and gave a playful smile. "Oh, I see." said Sonder, who expected more out of her. Then again, they were corsairs. At least, that was his assumption.

"So, what exactly do you guys do out here? Are you...*corsairs*?" Sonder asked Mason, becoming nervous of if a question like this was safe to ask. "Oh, we're not pirates or anything like that. More like...petty thieves just looking to...*get away from it all*." she answered and explained. "So you're drifters?" "Eh, I guess you could say that." Sonder thought this over for a moment and decided that it was at least a cut above them being corsairs.

"Does she have a name, your ship, I mean?" he found himself asking. "Oh, good question. Not really, actually. I couldn't even tell you the make of it. She's a family heirloom and an old girl, but she's gotten us where we're going time and time again—and damned fast too." said Mason. "So she's like a...*Nameless Maiden*, then?" Sonder asked. At this, Mason's deep-blue eyes shone with a brilliant flash, and she was suddenly speechless. "Wow. I like that...I think I'll use it! *The Nameless Maiden*. Huh. That's good." she said in response. Sonder chuckled at her enthusiasm for this idea.

"Wow, I had no idea that boys from different universes were so clever." she then said, causing Jasper and Klay to rush over and offer their protests. "Mason!" yelled Klay. Jasper groaned as his hand flew up to his forehead. At this, Mason paused the music, looked over at them and then returned her gaze to Sonder, and her eyes grew wide with horror. "Oh. Uh-oh." she said quietly. "Yeah, 'uh-oh.'" said Klay, who looked thoroughly unhappy with the girl.

"What?" Sonder asked with a blank expression. They had to be messing with him. Though, their reactions weren't exactly the joking kind. "What are you talking about?" Sonder asked them. "It's uh...nothing! We're just playing around." Mason explained, trying to play it off with a fake laugh that was entirely unconvincing. "Well, cat's out of the bag now, you might as well show him." said Klay, who then sighed loudly.

"Show me what?" Sonder asked. He was still very doubtful about what they were saying. But, there definitely had to be some truth to this, given the way everyone was acting. Jasper lifted a hand up to his face and shook his head slowly. "Well, uh...there's something you should probably know about us. It's kind of hard to believe, but, uh...we're *travelers from another universe*." Mason laid it all out flat for him.

Sonder was in total disbelief. He broke out of this by laughing, which continued for a minute or so before Klay cut in by saying: "See? He doesn't believe us." "Well, he's in for a surprise." said Jasper. "Mas', why don't you show the kid here some proof?" Klay asked Mason. "Oh, let me guess, you're going to put on some sort of fancy light show and have me smoke something that will 'allow me to see through the veil' or something." said Sonder in a mocking tone.

Klay shook his head with a sort of amusement at this. "Man, he's really asking for it." he then said. "Yep, guess we really have no other choice." Mason said with a playful smirk on her lips. "Oh boy, here we go." added Jasper, who took a seat and strapped himself in. Klay did the same. Ayb, following suit, returned to his station and re-assumed his cube form. Mason, ever the daring one, remained unbuckled in her chair.

"You might want to hold onto something." she then said to Sonder, who was still laughing. Tears escaped from the corners of his eyes. He really had been tickled pink by all this. "Make sure we only go into the safe ones this time." Klay said firmly. "I know, I know. Don't worry." said Mason, who then stood and reached up and drew down a strange rainbow ribbon like a seatbelt and connected it to a socket next to her. A strange, technological sound filled the air, and a multicolored light lit the floor and walls of the room in a similar fashion to Ayb's strip lights.

Then, Mason turned to Sonder and asked him, "Are you ready?" to which he replied, "Yeah, sure, go ahead." with a silly expression on his face. Then, Mason looked to Klay, who nodded, and she pulled back on a lever-switch atop her dashboard. Ahead of them, through the windshield of the ship, Sonder could see a strange, glowing rift of energy begin to form out in the frigid darkness.

Mason then put on a pair of brown leather gloves and pushed one of her control sticks forward, causing the ship to begin accelerating towards it. It was around this time that Sonder began to worry. *Were they really about to go into a different universe?* he asked himself. As they passed through the rift, Sonder could feel a slight tingle throughout his entire body, and the make-up of the ship around him seemed to jitter slightly. He had witnessed FTL Travel many times in his life, but this was something else entirely.

When they had arrived on the other side of the portal, Sonder could see that the space beyond them had taken on an amber coloration. Small, fluffy flecks of what looked like dust floated about freely around the ship. "Where are we?" Sonder asked, entranced by the view that was before him.

"Universe 3." Mason answered simply. Sonder turned and looked at her with an expression of doubt and slight mockery on his face.

"You have them numbered? Aren't they supposed to be of like an infinite quantity?" "You would think that, but actually, no. In fact, not a single one of them goes on completely forever as previously theorized, our probes have shown." Mason answered and then keyed in a few buttons on her control console. On one of the screens in front of her, a vector map of charted universes was shown. "If you look here, you can see that there are, give or take, thirteen observable *realms*." Mason said this in a very matter-of-factly way, but Sonder was still doubtful.

"Yeah? How'd you guys figure that out?" he asked. "Well, it's actually pretty simple. You see, when the Tech-Mages gifted these 'calculators'—or, *Rift Keys*—to the resistance network, we all set quickly to work on charting out a map of known space as quickly as we could." Jasper explained. Again, Sonder made a face. "Tech-Mages? Rift Keys? Okay, now you're definitely messing with me. I mean, this has to be just some far-off corner of the universe." he said as he gestured out through the windshield.

Mason looked at him with an expression of severity. "The Tech-Mages gave their lives to get us to where we are now." Sonder had definitely touched a nerve. "Oh, uh...okay." he then made a connection in his mind and decided to press his questioning. "Then why are you guys running? I mean, isn't that kind of like...*spitting in their faces*?"

Mason looked even more offended than she was before. "That's different." she said as she turned her gaze away from him. This was clearly a sore spot for her. "How is it different? I mean, if these guys had hope you'd help save this

'multiverse,' or whatever, then why didn't you—"
"Because that was before we knew the full picture." Mason looked Sonder dead in the eyes and cut him off sharply. "Full picture? What do you mean?"

"That we're doomed." she said with a cheery expression as she re-assumed her more outgoing side. Again, Sonder was stunned. "Oh. Uh. Okay then." he said as he turned away from her gaze. *Man, these people are crazy.* He thought to himself. It was then that another question bubbled up in his mind. "What exactly are you guys running from? You still haven't told me." he then asked the three corsairs, who looked amongst each other before looking over at Sonder.

"It's probably for the best that you don't know." said Jasper. Sonder was confused, and he felt like a child being kept in the dark. "Uh, okay...but I mean if it's really that dire, don't I at least have a right to know?" he then asked them. They looked as though they were stumped by this. "Nope." said Klay, firm as ever. "What? Why not?" Sonder pressed. "It's complicated, okay?" Klay reaffirmed his stance. Sonder sagged in his seat as his face took on a confused expression.

"Hey, in the meantime, why don't I show you some more proof?" offered Mason. Sonder turned to her and gave a slight nod in response. The pilot then pushed the lever-switch back to its original position, keyed in a few buttons next to it, then pulled back on the lever once again. Another rift appeared ahead of the ship, and once they were through it, Sonder could see what looked like a world made of fluctuating and reticulating mirrors all around them through the windshield.

"Whoa..." he said aloud. "Universe 4." Mason stated as she gestured to the outside world. Sonder was mesmerized, but he still wasn't entirely convinced. "So, this is a full universe, right? Like, it's got planets and stuff? Entire galaxies?" he asked. "Yes. Well, at least, it has equivalents of that. Not all universes are created equal. Some are big, some small. Just depends. Even the way things fundamentally function can be different. Life here grows on those mirror plates much in the same way that it does on planetoids. The source of light here is actually caused by the diffusion of trillions of these tiny, microscopic shards of glass that are superheated by—"

"Okay, now that's just ridiculous. How does anything like this form naturally?" Sonder cut the professor (Jasper) off and asked. This caused a playful smirk to cut across Mason's face as her eyes narrowed. "I don't know, man. You tell me." she answered, putting her hands behind her head as she sunk further into her chair.

"Does this mean this all has some kind of...intelligent design to it?" "Maybe. I dunno, I just work here." "So then, somewhere along the way, you guys must have discovered evidence of '*God*,' right?" Sonder asked. Jasper, Klay, and Mason exchanged a look between each other. "Whoa...that's a heavy question." said Mason. "That's way above our paygrade. It wasn't exactly our job to investigate something like that. We were kind of too busy in our recruiting efforts and exploring of options. That's something you should ask the higher-ups, if you get the chance. Though, with us deserting the cause, I'm not so sure they'd want to hear from us." explained Jasper, who looked as though he were eager to move on from the subject.

This was a sound argument, but Sonder couldn't help but feel a little bit miffed at this. "Do you guys gloss over everything?" he asked the trio.

"It's kind of our stock-and-trade, honestly." said Mason. "Makes things easier, if you ask me." she continued. Sonder started to develop a slight headache from trying to think all of this through, but he decided that it ultimately wasn't worth it to press his questions or waste his already strained brain power on such topics for the time being. One day, he hoped, he would have all the answers to the great mysteries in his life.

It was then that another question dawned on him. "Wait, so, how is any of this possible? Like, what's the secret to jumping universes? Or realms, or whatever." he asked Mason. "Oh, it's real simple, actually: *you just divide by zero.*" she answered with a playful look on her face.

Sonder was completely dumbfounded. Jasper and Klay were also thoroughly amused by this, as if it were some kind of inside joke. "Now, existential questions aside, are you ready for some real fun?" she asked him. "Uh, sure. I think my brain's becoming mushy from all this, though." Mason laughed at this. "Oh, we're only just getting started." she then said.

. . .

What followed next was a rollercoaster of an experience. Mason flew them through various parts of the universes, each bearing their own unique brand of what the word meant. Though many resembled the one that Sonder was familiar with, there were a great deal that perplexed him and nearly broke his mind. He almost lost his lunch when they visited a world that existed solely in the second dimension.

Another one in particular showcased a world wracked by constant, ceaseless war. The planets and stars themselves had been shaped into what Sonder equated to warships, as if each one had been transformed by their inhabitants for the sole purpose of waging warfare. Stray blasts of energy tore past the ship like bolts of lightning, but thanks to Mason's precise piloting capabilities, they never once got hit. The ones waging the war were too caught up in the moment to notice a ship as small as the *Maiden*. "Okay, I think I get the idea, please get us out of here!" Sonder yelled. "Aww, but this is so much fun!" Mason hollered back before loosing a few loud laughs. "Did you guys try to recruit these people?" Sonder asked. "Yeah, it didn't go so well.' answered Klay. Mason then opened up a final rift and guided the ship through it.

When they arrived on the other side, they found themselves in a world of black mist. Far off, in the center of their view, was what looked like a ring of enormous golden crystals that appeared to be acting as a sort of protective fencing around a small system of floating plateaus, each paired with a smaller crystal. The giant gems were being smothered by some sort of black sinew-like material that seemed to be siphoning their light.

"Whoa, where are we?" Sonder asked. It was then that an electrical surge crackled through the ship and the lighting inside the cabin flickered and then died out entirely. Then, the emergency auxiliary power system switched on, filling the room with a dull, orange light. "Uh-oh." said Mason. "What's 'uh-oh?' Did we run out of gas or something?" asked Sonder. "No, the ship runs on vaporized water." Klay explained. "Ayb, where are we?" Mason asked the synthform. "We are in *his domain*." the large, talking cube explained. Though the synthform spoke in monotone, Sonder could detect a sense of dire warning in his words.

A tense, cold silence filled the air like a deathly miasma. Suddenly, in the gloomy dark of the ship's cabin, Sonder began to give off a faint glow that the crew took notice of. "Whoa..." said Klay, who looked at Sonder with a sense of reverence. "What? What is it?" Sonder asked, feeling somewhat creeped out and apprehensive about the sudden attention he was receiving from everyone. "You're *glowing*." Klay answered.

Though it wasn't enough to completely illuminate the cockpit-bridge, it certainly was noticeable enough to comment on. Sonder looked down at his hands, and surely enough, he, too, noticed the faint, iridescent glow coming off of his skin. "What the...?" he asked aloud as confusion entered his mind. Klay then returned his attention to their situation.

"Mason, get us out of here." "I would love to, but—" "But what?" Klay asked, sounding antsy.

"The engine's offline." The answer didn't seem to thrill anyone. "We must have made too many jumps too quickly and it sent us off-course before running out of juice." Mason explained. "Well, let's get it fixed, then!" barked Klay, who quickly unbuckled himself from his seat and led Mason as they rushed towards the cabin's door.

It was then that the door to the bridge slid open, prompting everyone to freeze in place. Standing in the doorway was a man dressed in all black. He had a wide-brimmed hat, long, curly dark-brown hair, and a stylish mustache and a pointed beard adorning his face. In one of his black-gloved hands, he held a glass bottle of amber-colored alcohol. A black trench coat clung loosely to his shoulders.

"What's with all the racket?" he asked the group in a gruff voice that had an exotic accent to it. He sounded as though he had been drinking for some time. "Sorry to wake you, sir." Jasper apologized. "No, it's quite alright. I've been out for too long. There's more drink to consume." he said with the same playful enthusiasm as a drunken party animal as he lifted the open bottle to his lips and threw back another swig.

Mason made a small sound of disapproval at this. Klay walked over to the man, and Sonder got a sense of just how tall he was, as he completely dwarfed the rusty-red-haired man. "Alright, Cap'n, that's enough for now." said Klay as he tried to take away the bottle from the man, who pulled it away from his reach. "Don't worry, I know when to stop." he said rather drunkenly before burping loudly. "It's a solution, not a problem, eh?" he asked everyone else in the room with an enthusiastic, upbeat expression on his face that made him appear very silly. Jasper and Mason gave the man a sympathetic look at this.

"Now tell me, my friends, where are we?" he asked them. "We're in 13, sir." Mason answered him. "13? Why go there?" the man asked as his eyes widened slightly. "It wasn't our idea, sir, it's just where we ended up." Mason explained before turning her attention to the Rift Key. She knelt back down and continued working on it. At this point, the man started to move towards them in a swaying fashion. He stopped just in front of Sonder, who had to crane his neck to look up at him. "And who might this be?" he asked, looking down at him with a raised eyebrow. His brown eyes looked dull and glazed-over. "That's Sonder, we uh, we picked him up during our last supply run." explained Jasper. "Ayb crushed him like a can, and we felt bad, so we healed him up and brought him with us." Mason helped to explain.

"Sonder, huh? Sonder...?" he asked, probing for a last name. "It's just Sonder." Jasper answered. This made the tall, dark man smirk as he made a connection. "So we've got one man who only goes by his last name, and now one who only goes by his first. Interesting." he then said, chuckling. "Well met. I take it *Red* was the one giving orders, then?" he asked in general as he turned and faced Klay, giving him a look of disapproval. "Yeah, it's on me." said Klay. "Hmm." grumbled the man. "In any case, welcome aboard, *Snow*." "Uh, *Snow*?" Sonder asked. "Don't worry about that, the Captain likes to give us these little names. You'll get used to it." Jasper explained. "That's quite right, *Doc*." said the man as he turned to face Jasper. "Oh, uh, okay." said Sonder. Jasper stepped over to the two of them as Klay moved in to help Mason.

"Uh, sorry, this is Captain—" "Ozomatli Raizar, at your service, my good friend." the drunken man finished answering for Jasper and extended his hand out towards Sonder. "Uh, nice to meet you, Mr. Raizar, sir." said Sonder, who held his hand out nervously as he looked up at the man. "Please, call me 'Ozo.'" Raizar said with a grin as he took Sonder's hand and gave it a firm shake. "*Fates*, why is it so dark in here?" he then asked. "We were just about to fix that, come on, Klay." urged Mason, who then rushed past Raizar with the rusty-red-haired man in tow and out into the hallway, where they quickly opened up the floor hatch and climbed down the ladder beneath it into the ship's engine room.

"Seems like quite a lot has happened since I've been out." said Raizar, who looked strangely impressed. It was then that a familiar shape wandered in behind the captain. The four-footed wolf-like beastie wore a curious expression as it looked over at Sonder with its head turned slightly. Its three tails lowered as it took on a more stiff and timid demeanor. Raizar took notice of the animal and knelt down slowly next to him. "Oh, Maelo, I see you're up from your nap, old boy." he said as he began to gently stroke its sleek, black fur. "Go on then, this here's our new guest." Raizar then said as he gestured to Sonder.

The animal walked over to him with a slow and cautious step. Sonder felt a slight sense of tension as the beast moved towards him. Carefully, he extended his hand out slowly, allowing the animal to sniff him. As it did this, its tails lifted back up and started to wag. The wolf-like creature then rose to its full height as its ears raised up, and it loosed a loud *WOOF!* that startled Sonder. The animal began to pant as its face took on a happy expression. "Oh-ho-ho, I think he likes you. Go on then." Raizar encouraged the animal, and it moved closer to Sonder and started licking at his face and arms (which were uncovered by his rolled-up sleeves), drawing out a laugh from him. "Good boy, Maelo, good boy!" said Raizar. The wolf-like creature's red eyes were dazzling up close.

Sonder pet the animal for a moment, which only caused it to become even more excited. "What is he, exactly?" Sonder then asked as he looked up at the captain. "He's a *vector wolf*. We picked him up during our travels. He's been our best companion." Raizar explained. Ayb let loose a disapproving beep-like sound at this. "Oh, hush up, you old synthform. You're great, too." Raizar said to the blue-plated box. "I remember seeing lots of him back on the train, unless it's just my memory acting up on me." Sonder explained as he rubbed at his head.

"Oh, well, you see, that's sort-of his specialty; vector wolves have a pretty magical ability to multiply or bud-off into dozens and sometimes even hundreds of its own kind and then morphs all back together into one body. I don't exactly know how it's possible, but he just does it." explained Raizar. "It's certainly come in handy during our runs, that's for sure." he continued.

"Huh. Weird." said Sonder, causing Maelo to cock his head slightly to the side and whine in a curious tone as though he understood this. Just as Sonder was about to question the crew's thieving habits, the ship's proximity alarm sounded suddenly, and the cabin of the cockpit-bridge was flooded with flashing red light. The blaring klaxon was jolting for Sonder to hear, and he quickly threw his hands over his ears to block out the noise.

"What's going on?!" he asked, having to yell over it. Mason and Klay rushed back into the room in a frantic flutter, and the pilot quickly re-assumed her seated position and switched off the alarm. Looking over the display screens on the dashboard, she indicated a ship's presence closing in on their position on the radar. "There. Something's coming." said Mason. "Damn it, could it be *them*?" Klay asked, sounding fearful.

"I'm not sure. It's not moving like any of *their* ships." Mason explained. Jasper looked frightened as he knelt down and held Maelo tightly close to him. "Ms. Vohldt, can you get us moving?" Captain Raizar asked. "I had just enough time to get the engine started again, but we're only at half power." she explained with palpable fear in her voice.

Then, a noise sounded from outside the ship, prompting everyone's attention. "What was that?" asked Sonder. A moment later, he had his answer. From out of the unfolding darkness came a monstrosity that had a grin like that of a shark. Its completely rusted and crudely-assembled shape was smeared with a dark red coloration. Everyone in the *Nameless Maiden*'s cabin was taken by the sight of it. The glowing flames of torches danced about in the crude ship's windows, their light bouncing off of the mist around both crafts. As the shark-like ship's tooth-like maw opened slowly to receive them, panic began to set in as it drew closer.

"They're not getting me without a fight." said Mason with a fierce determination as she took the control sticks of the vehicle into her gloved hands and swung the ship around before slamming her foot onto the gas pedal. The boosters kicked in, sending the ship forward at a fast rate. Just then, the craft shook hard as something impacted onto it, and it was stopped dead in its tracks. Outside, a piercing anchor connected to a chain had been shot out and was embedded into the hull of the

Nameless Maiden. It had started to pull them into the mouth of the larger ship.

"Dammit, they've got us!" yelled Mason, who pushed the pedal even harder. When she found that this wasn't working, she withdrew her foot. Captain Raizar roused Ayb with the press of a few small buttons on a wrist-worn device and barked an order: "Ayb, initiate security protocols!" he yelled, sounding as though he had sobered up suddenly in the moment. The robotic being switched back on, rose to its full height, and its wrists and shoulders opened up to reveal internal, long-barreled guns and a saw blade. It then took on a defensive stance and braced with the others as the *Nameless Maiden* was pulled into the rusty ship's maw.

A moment later, it touched down hard onto a crude metal floor, jostling everyone in the cabin around. After getting back up to their feet, the crew and Sonder looked about at each other with pulsing fear in their eyes. Then, it sounded like great chains were being heaped up over the body of the ship. Soon after, the ship's inhabitants could hear what sounded like maniacal and fiendish laughter coming from all around, encroaching upon them fast.

"Is this what you guys have been running from?" Sonder asked Raizar. There was an air of seriousness about the captain that seemed to indicate a far more dire reality. "No. This is something else. *Saurossians.*" he explained as they all (save for Sonder) drew out their guns, which varied in size and style. Ayb reassumed his battle-stance and got lined up with the others, who could hear what sounded like the ramp of the ship being forced open, and the craft started to shake slightly as several somethings boarded it.

"Here they come." Mason said, trying to keep her cool as best she could in this situation. Maelo tucked his tails under himself as he let out a whine before disappearing somewhere in the cockpit-bridge, likely finding a good place to hide. The metal flooring of the ship groaned around them as its weight limit was being reached, and the shaking became gradually more intense.

Then, everything became deathly still, and all they could hear was their breathing. It happened in a moment—dozens, no possibly hundreds of tall, reptilian humanoids with scarlet scales and crude gems for eyes poured in through the sliding door of the bridge and overwhelmed the crew, letting out maniacal laughs as they overtook them. Though they had each fired off a handful of rounds, this effort was wasted, as they hadn't managed to take down more than a few of them before being overwhelmed...

Stage II:

Dread Nought

The next thing Sonder knew, he was being dragged by his arms down a blood-red, flame-lit hallway that looked as though it were made up of sewn-together bits of various other ships. Around him was a sea of marching crimson scales. Whoever, or whatever these things were, they were far from human, and yet they walked as though they were people. To his left and right, he could barely make out the shapes of the others as they, too, were being brought up the crude corridor.

Sonder wished desperately to cry out for the others, but fear had overtaken him completely, choking his vocal chords and keeping him from making a single sound. Soon enough, they had arrived at their destination, evidenced by the horde of Saurossians coming to a stop. Sonder threw his head back and though he was upside-down, he could see that they were before a pair of large doors that were decorated with various ivory trophy skulls. These were pulled open by a pair of guards that wore mismatched metal helmets (likely pilfered from previous victims), and the sight of some sort of throne room was revealed.

Having to look past several scaly legs, Sonder could partly make out what appeared to be padded floors that were populated by the forms of a few dozen Saurossians that were either in the throes of mating or killing each other, a sight that shocked Sonder to his core. Sounds of pain and pleasure poured out of the room and into the hall. In the center, sat on high on a lavish-looking throne was an albino Saurossian that had one of its legs propped up over the other, and in one hand it held a glass filled with wine or blood that it swished about gently before raising it to its scaly lips and drawing a small mouthful from it.

Then, Sonder felt himself being lifted up over the heads of the Saurossians that were carrying him. They rushed forward and then threw him and the others down before the pale reptilian humanoid, who sat up and rose from their regal seat. Fighting through waves of pain, Sonder raised himself up onto his elbows and looked around, finding Raizar and the others to his left and right.

He then flicked his eyes up to the albino creature, who walked over to them with a snake-like gracefulness, its hips swaying sensually as it approached. It wore a long, purple skirt, a golden bandolier covered up its breasts, and it had mismatched golden earrings that hung from below its hearing holes. Up close, its long face resembled a snake's more than a lizards, and its scaly skin looked smooth, unlike the rough, bumpy kind that the Saurossians that carried them in had. Atop its head were a pair of red gems that appeared to act as eyes of some sort. Then, it began to speak in hisses that Sonder could not understand. Though, its body language and hand movements seemed to indicate a sense of purpose and structure to the way it was talking.

Sonder turned to Raizar, whose eyes were filled with disoriented rage as they were fixed on those of the albino's. Finding that he couldn't catch the captain's gaze, Sonder then turned to the other side, where he found Jasper, who was worse for wear. He had a bloody nose, a split lip, and bruising on one of his cheeks, and he had lost his glasses at some point. His clothing had also been torn in a few places, and his emerald-green eyes were full of pain, fear, and sadness. It ate at Sonder, who then was overcome with a boiling hatred for the Saurossians. Beyond Jasper and Raizar, Sonder could see that Mason, Klay, and Ayb were all in similar shape.

He didn't know whether to feel relieved or worried that he couldn't find Maelo anywhere, deciding that he hoped he had either gotten away or found a good place to hide on the *Nameless Maiden*. The albino continued to hiss and gesture with its sharp-nailed hands, which were strangely human in a way for a good while before it gave a final hiss and a snap of its fingers.

Then, Sonder felt himself get wrenched up onto his feet by powerful, scaly arms before he was dragged off into a darker, much more narrow hallway that was to the left inside of the throne room. As he was being moved, he could see that the others shared a similar fate, save for Mason, who had been left alone before the albino, who reached down and grabbed the girl by her chin, something that deeply angered and upset Sonder to see. He kicked and fought against the Saurossians that were carrying him, but to no avail. His reward was a hard gut punch from one of the guards. The pain from this made him black out on the spot.

Hours later, Sonder awoke and found himself inside a crudely-assembled metal-barred cell with a stone top, and a technological lock held its door shut. Around and across from him were identical cells that appeared to be empty. He peeled himself from off the cold, rusted-over metal flooring and looked about in the cell, finding that he had been lumped in with the others (save for Mason).

Ayb was switched off and had a large dent in his camera-like head. Jasper was rocking back and forth, and tears poured down his face like streams of river water as he clung to Klay, who comforted him. Raizar, who was also seated, appeared to be in a sort of defeated trance as he drunkenly swayed gently in place.

"Guys?" Sonder asked aloud, finding that it hurt his diaphragm to speak, and his throat was mighty dry. This prompted Jasper and Klay to look over at him, and the boyish young man loosed from Klay and embraced Sonder tightly as he shook and sobbed over him. "We thought you were dead, man." Klay said simply, sounding as though any sense of fight had left him long ago.

"I'm so sorry, I'm so sorry..." Jasper kept repeating as he clutched onto him like a frightened child. Sonder didn't have the faintest idea of what to say or do in response to all of this. Then, a sense of purpose came over him, and he said simply: "We need to save Mason." Though this was something they all agreed on, they hadn't the first clue as to how to go about this. "Look, I'm with you, but how exactly are *we* going to do that?" Klay asked him. Sonder wracked his mind, which throbbed with exhaustion, pain, and dehydration.

"You guys must have experience with picking locks, right?" Sonder asked. "We thought of that already, but..." Klay started to say, then gestured outside the cell, where there were Saurossians that had what looked like spears and automatic weapons pacing up and down the cell block. "I don't wanna lose any fingers or a hand to these bastards." Klay finished explaining.

Sonder sank at this, then asked: "So what are these things, anyway?" "*Saurossians*. At least, that's what the resistance network calls them. They're scavengers from one of the realms. They stole some of our Rift Keys and have been going through each of the worlds, stealing and killing, and doing what cold, unfeeling reptiles like them do best. Though, I'm not sure why they'd want to stick around for long in a place like 13." Klay explained. "We had some pretty good luck until today." he added. Sonder couldn't help but feel a bit stung by this.

"Sorry, it's not your fault we're in this mess. We just got a little too careless." said Klay, remedying his previous statement. Jasper hugged Sonder even tighter. "Hey, Jasper, you okay?" Sonder then asked him with raspy vocal chords as he gave Jasper's arm a couple of pats. At first, there was no answer, but a moment later, he straightened up and sniffled before saying: "This is all just...this is hell. I'm so sorry we dragged you along, Sonder." as he dried his reddened eyes. Reflecting on the entirety of the life he had known, Sonder was entirely sick of having his freedom stripped from him, to have others step over him and control what he did. It was about time that he took matters into his own hands sand pushed back against the world. Feeling determined to get out of this predicament, Sonder stiffened up and said: "Hey, can't really do much about the past, now can we? I mean, we're here. So, let's figure a way out of this mess. Sound good?" to which Jasper gave a feverish series of nods as he continued to snuffle.

"Sheesh, sounds like you've got a real pair on you, Sonder. So, what's the plan, big man?" Klay asked him. Sonder thought for a moment, then answered. "Can we get Ayb back online?" "I'll see what I can do." Klay responded before crouch-walking over to the synthform (as the ceiling of the cell was quite low, seeming to have been designed to shame its inhabitants prior to whatever it was the Saurossians did with them) and setting quickly to work on trying to reactivate it.

"Jasper, do you have any pins on you? Any small bits of metal or anything?" Sonder asked the platinum-haired young man. "I can't see...I'll have to feel around..." the medic lamented in a snuffy tone as he patted himself over until he found a pocket that he unzipped to reveal a handful of pin-clasped rolls of gauze. "Will these do?" Jasper asked in a small voice as he pulled out and showcased one of the pins. The beat-up green-eyed boy was squinting in order to see in the dimly lit brig. Sonder gave an encouraging smile at this. "Those will work perfectly. Thank you." he said before giving him a firm pat on his shoulder.

Then, Sonder moved closer to the captain, who continued to sway. He was completely oblivious to the world around him. Sonder first tried to wave his hand in front of his face to try and catch his eye, but this failed. Sonder then grabbed him by the shoulder and shook him slightly. When this, too, didn't work, Sonder shook him even harder, until Raizar snapped to attention and turned to face him with his brown eyes opened wide. "Raizar?" Sonder asked.

The captain's mouth wagged open, and it looked as if he was struggling to find his tongue. "I'm...a coward." The words seared straight through Sonder. "I got us into this mess because...because I gave into my fears...and we all ran..." Raizar continued explaining. Sonder searched his mind for an appropriate response to this, and after taking a deep breath, he said to Raizar: "Look, I have no idea what you guys are dealing with; whatever it is you're running from. But, right now, we need a leader. We need *Captain Ozomatli Raizar*."

Hearing his name made him perk up slowly, and he pressed his crumpled-up wide-brimmed black hat more firmly onto his head before turning to look around and assess the situation. He then faced Sonder with a gleaming look in his eye and a smirk and said: "Alright, my friend. We're going to do this." Filled with a renewed sense of hope, Klay worked faster, and Captain Raizar helped Jasper and Sonder with trying to pick the lock. They had to do it in shifts so as to avoid the gem-eyed gaze of the guards. Unfortunately, one of them took notice of the fact that they were tampering with the lock and walked slowly over to them as it began to huff and puff with frustration.

The guard then unlocked the cage, threw open its door, and snatched Sonder from it before slamming it shut and locking it once more. Holding him up with its free hand (the other was holding a plasma repeater), the Saurossian guard started to choke the life out of Sonder. As this went on, Jasper cried out for the guard to release him, and Klay began to shout at it.

Then, its grip tightened around his throat as it began to hiss something in its native tongue at him. As his consciousness wavered, Sonder's glow became increasingly brighter to a point where it was nearly blinding to look at. Then, a great flash of energy went out from Sonder, splashing the room with heat. The guard and the other Saurossians around it were burnt to a crisp by the surge and it dropped Sonder on the spot as it keeled over dead. The electrics in the locks of every nearby cell were fried, allowing the others to escape. Sonder massaged his throat as he looked around in a dazed state of confusion.

"What was that?" Klay asked Sonder as he pushed open the cell's door and exited it with Jasper and Captain Raizar in tow. "I...I have no idea." Sonder answered honestly. "I've never seen anything like that..." Jasper said as he looked down at Sonder with his eyes full of concern. Sonder mistook this for Jasper looking at him as though he were some kind of freak show. The short young man extended a hand out to Sonder and reassured him by saying: "I'm grateful you had something like that in your back pocket."

Sonder took his hand, and Jasper lifted him up from the ground. Klay picked up the guard's weapon and looked it over, quickly determining how it worked. "Great, so where do we go now? We don't exactly have enough weapons for all of us. Not to mention, Ayb's still out of commission." asked Klay. "We'll find some. We have to." said Captain Raizar, who was alive with a burning vigor that brought everyone's mood upward, and their faith in pulling this off became stronger.

"*Red, Snow*, you'll have to carry Ayb. Let's get our pilot back and get the hell out of here." he said firmly as he took the lead. Sonder was impressed by this sudden surge of confidence, and hoped that he would never stop running with it. Klay and Sonder then retrieved the mechanical being from the cell and dragged his body behind them. Its metal frame was very heavy, causing both men to groan every so often from the effort it took to carry him.

They moved past several emptied cells that were stained with dried, old blood. Just as they were about to clear the block, Sonder caught a glimpse of someone sitting alone in a cell. He could barely make out their sleek, messy black hair, which hid their face and hung down past their knobby knees. Black striping, much like that of a wild's cat, covered the length of their pale-white skin like a tattoo. It seemed to him that the humanoid occupant must have been imprisoned for a great deal of time, indicated by how deathly thin and ragged they appeared.

"Wait, guys. Look." Sonder said as he gestured to the cell, prompting them all to stop in their tracks and turn back to get a look. "Who is that?" asked Klay. "I don't know, but I think we should break them out." Sonder said back. He and Klay put Ayb down for the time being, and Sonder knelt down and took the technological lock in his hands, finding that it had been melted in a way that made it impossible to open with a key. They had been left to rot by their captors.

"You really think that's a good idea? We should probably just get out of here. Don't forget, Mason's still in trouble." said Klay. "They might help us though." Sonder said firmly. "Don't worry, we'll get you out of there." he then reaffirmed to the cell's inhabitant as he took the lock in his hands and closed his eyes as he focused on trying to channel his hidden powers. Through his closed eyelids, he could see an increasing glow coming from right in front of him.

As he opened his eyes, he could see that it was coming from his hands, which began to superheat the lock. After a few seconds, the lock melted away before them. "Whoa..." exclaimed Klay. Then, the glow grew dimmer until it was back to the state it had been in. Sonder was at a loss for words. "How are you doing that?" asked Captain Raizar, who exchanged looks with Klay and Jasper. "I...I don't know." replied Sonder, who looked over his hands with widened eyes. The prisoner raised their head to look at them, revealing a set of cat-like golden eyes behind the mess of black hair that obscured their identity.

Then, in a blinding flash, they tore out of the cell and rushed past Sonder and the others, toppling them all over. "Hey, wait!" Sonder called out to them, but they refused to stop, disappearing into the dark depths of the Saurossian ship. "Damn it, they went completely the other way. Think we should follow them?" Klay asked Captain Raizar. "I think we should. Come on, hurry!" he answered as he kicked up into as fast of a run as he could manage. The others followed closely after him with Ayb in tow.

Just as they reached the other side, they were stopped dead in their tracks by a Saurossian guard that was armed with an automatic plasma repeater, which it activated by cocking the priming pump on its bottom with its powerful hands. It hissed out a command of sorts, likely for them to return to their cage or suffer the consequences. Klay raised the stolen repeater and aimed it at the guard as the others braced themselves.

Just before either Klay or the guard could get a shot off, the shape of the prisoner they freed launched out of the shadows at the speed of a cracking whip and landed onto the guard hard, tackling them to the ground, where they then took its toothy head into their hands and repeatedly slammed it onto the floor of the cell block until it became severely bloodied. Then, the escapee, in a shocking move, twisted and tore the guard's head off. Blood dripped from its severed head and the stump it once belonged to.

Then, the striped prisoner threw the head across the room and disappeared once more into the shadows. Sonder and the others were shocked and speechless. "Well, looks like they're on our side, then." Sonder said. Klay made a face of horrified disgust after witnessing the display of violence. "I'm not sure, we should be careful. From what we've seen so far, they seem like some sort of *killing freak*. Maybe there was a reason they were locked up." said Klay, his words making everyone weary. Sonder considered this, but stuck to being hopeful.

Jasper looked as though he were about to be sick. Captain Raizar picked up the second guard's weapon and then led them up the crude, rusty stairs. "Come on, let's move!" he exclaimed as they rushed up through the gloom of the stairway. "How are you holding up, Cap'n?" Klay called up to him as they ran. "I'm doing okay. Drinks are on me when we get back to the ship." answered Captain Raizar, who also kept running. This drew a laugh out of Klay, who then said: "You've really got to take it easy on the booze, man."

This made Raizar chuckle. Sonder felt relieved to hear them acting like they normally seemed to. He was also hopeful that they wouldn't have to carry Ayb for much longer, as the weight of the synthform was beginning to tire him out. When they got to the top of the stairs, they found themselves in a wide hallway with uneven doorways on each side.

Suddenly, a Saurossian appeared from out of one of these rooms, causing everyone to stop dead in their tracks. Klay dropped Ayb, took aim, and fired off a shot that bored into the creature's shoulder, melting away its red, scaly flesh and causing it to roar in pain. The Saurossian then turned and aimed its weapon at Klay. But, just in the nick of time, the striped prisoner dropped from the ceiling onto the reptilian humanoid, causing it to fall to the ground. In the prisoner's hand was a sharpened metal pipe that they must have tore away from the ship's interior hull.

They raised the makeshift weapon and began to pummel the Saurossian with it. They were hitting them so hard with it that the others could hear the metal reverberating off of its skull. One bloody, brainy mess later, the prisoner cast aside the bent-up pipe and replaced it with a large knife that the Saurossian had sheathed at its side before launching towards the other Saurossians that had come out of the rooms of the hall. Within moments, the prisoner had made short work of them, unleashing even more of the fury that they must have been building up during their imprisonment.

Despite their ragged and bone-thin appearance, they had the might and bloodlust of a fully-rested and well-fed warrior. Just when Sonder and the others thought that the prisoner was about to get nabbed by the Saurossians, who had ganged up on them, the striped escapee tore out of their grip and shredded them all up with the knife; gutting them and slicing their throats in a whirlwind-like fashion.

It was an artful display of martial prowess and shedding blood.

The prisoner stood for a moment and reflected on their kills, reveling in what they had done before once again disappearing into the shadows of the ship, knife still in hand. Before vanishing completely from sight, they looked back at Sonder and the others with their golden eyes as she ran. Witnessing this, Klay was slightly more convinced that the prisoner was looking out for them. Still, their excessively violent nature was hard to stomach. "Sheesh, that was close." remarked Sonder. "Come on, let's keep moving!" Captain Raizar yelled, and the rusty-red-haired man moved over to quickly help Sonder with carrying Ayb again. "Wait! Mason might be being held in one of these rooms." said Jasper, who then looked through each one as they moved, but found that these led to larger spaces with more

Saurossians, "Wrong one!" (he yelled before quickly shutting its door once more), or to spaces where the creatures stored their spoils and meat supply.

One room in particular caught Jasper's eye, though, leading to him stepping inside and investigating it. It was filled with various bits and bobs of stolen tech. There was a small tablet resting above the rest of the junk that looked to be of similar origin in terms of design as the Rift Key they had back on the *Maiden*. Jasper took it into his hands and looked it over. The screen switched on at his touch, and what he found on it made his eyes widen. He then looked behind it to find his glasses, which were bent-up and in need of repairs. A sense of relief washed over him. "Come on, Jasper, we gotta move!" Klay called to him as the Saurossians from one of the rooms had started to open fire on them. Captain Raizar and Klay engaged them in a gunfight, trading searing-hot bolts of plasma with the reptilian humanoids.

Jasper then quickly pocketed the device, placed his glasses back over his face (they luckily still fit), rushed out of the room, and rejoined the others, who had managed to take out the Saurossians with their weapons. The group then made their way through the rest of the hall, having to step over the bodies of the Saurossians that the striped prisoner left in their wake, and moved quickly up the stairs. Soon enough, they found their way back inside the throne room. Streaks of blood-spray colored the walls, floors and cushions. But, there was no sign of Mason, the escaped prisoner, or the Albino Alpha.

"Man, what a mess. Do they not know the meaning of restraint?" asked Klay. "Hey, they cleaned up house for us. I'm grateful. Makes things much easier for us. Look!" said Captain Raizar, who then dropped Ayb and indicated more of the Saurossian's looted weapons, which Jasper and Sonder picked up and armed themselves. The captain found his revolver among the bodies.

"There you are, my darling. Good to have you back." he said quietly to the gun and then kissed it. "Watch out!" yelled Klay, and Captain Raizar tackled Sonder in the direction of the throne, taking cover behind it as bolts of plasma energy and bullets tore through the air right next to them. Jasper, Klay, and Ayb took refuge back in the stairwell's entry. "How many of 'em are there?" Klay called out to the captain, who braced himself, steeled his courage, and then peered out around the throne for a brief second before returning very quickly to the safety behind the bullet-proof chair as another volley of metal and energy blasted past him.

"I count twenty!" hollered Captain Raizar. "You sure you're seein' right, old man?!" Klay called out to him. This made Raizar smile and chuckle. "I'm completely dry, trust me my friend!" Captain Raizar yelled in reply. By now, they were all smiling, save for Jasper, who was not having any semblance of a good time at all. The motley crew of the *Nameless Maiden* prepared themselves for the shoot-out, with each one of them drawing in a deep breath. Sonder could feel his heart practically leaping out of his chest from the adrenaline.

Just as the captain was about to pop out and fire off the first replying round, the striped prisoner appeared and sliced straight across the lined-up Saurossians' throats with the knife, coming to a sliding stop just before hitting the wall. Their bodies dropped limply to the floor. It had happened so fast that Captain Raizar could have blinked and he would have missed it. With an impressed look on his face, the captain rose up and out from the hiding spot behind the throne with a cautious step. The prisoner fixed him a withering glare before turning and running out through the opened double doors. "Man, they must really hate these things." said Klay as he looked over the fresh bodies.

"Well, you probably would too if you were held prisoner here as long as they seem to have been." said Sonder, who was very relieved that he hadn't needed to fire off the weapon in his hands. "Let's keep moving, Mason could be anywhere in this rusted hulk." said Captain Raizar, who then led them out of the room through the double doors and into the big hall they had been dragged through. The large space was now littered with bodies and loot, some of which Klay in particular helped himself to.

"What? It's not like they'll be needing this stuff anymore." he said in his defense. "Yeah, but it'd be nice if you wouldn't pause every few seconds to grab something; this big hunk of metal is a pain to carry." said Sonder, who was growing very tired of lugging Ayb around. "Come on, Mason, where are you?" Captain Raizar asked aloud in a quiet voice as he looked about the room they were in.

"The ship's through here." said Jasper, who indicated the door at the end of the hall, and they all followed him as he went through it. Before them was the *Nameless Maiden*, which had been bound up by giant chains. The anchor-spear was still embedded in its top, and beyond it were the closed jaws of the large hangar door. Littered about were the cut-apart remains of starships and weaponry. "Good call, *Doc*." said Captain Raizar, who gave Jasper a firm pat on the shoulder. They had all lost their sense of direction when they were first captured, especially with them being surrounded by Saurossians. Jasper had been the only one to take a mental note of where exactly they had all been moved from.

It was then that they took notice of the Albino Alpha walking out from behind storage crates with Mason in her clutches. It was holding a knife to her throat. Captain Raizar signaled for everyone to stop where they were.

"Wait!" he yelled in a commanding tone that boomed like thunder. Then, he and the Alpha locked eyes. The crystals appeared to take on a fiercer shape. Its lips were pulled up in a snarling fashion, and a series of hisses loosed from behind its needle-like teeth. Mason looked at the others with widened, tear-streaked deep-blue eyes. Her wavy, blonde locks were a mess, and her clothes had been partially torn up by the Alpha. Fear had seized her entirely.

"Let's not do anything too hasty, now." Captain Raizar urged the Saurossian, who responded with more hisses. Then, from out of the shadows, the striped prisoner leapt at the Alpha, tackling both it and Mason to the ground in a blur. Instinctively, the prisoner quickly separated Mason from the Alpha, who then stabbed into the prisoner's leg as it attempted to get Mason with it.

The striped escapee howled in pain and retreated from the Alpha. Mason scrambled over to the others, who received her warmly as they witnessed the Alpha get up and stare down the prisoner. It gave the others a nasty look but quickly turned its attention back to the prisoner, who stepped slowly towards it. "'Bout time you guys showed up." said Mason as waves of relief crashed over them all. "Where's Maelo?" Captain

Raizar asked. "I think he's still aboard the ship." explained Mason. The prisoner's golden eyes gleamed with rage as they stared into the gem-like protrusions above the Alpha's head.

Then, in a flash, they both charged each other and traded slices with their knives. "Move, now!" ordered Captain Raizar, and he led the others around the fight and over to the captured ship. They set to work quickly on freeing the craft from its chains, having to climb the storage crates to get on top of it. Meanwhile, the prisoner and the Alpha clashed like pouncing wild beasts, with both of them managing to get cuts in on the other. Blood trickled down each of their bodies from the wounds as they breathed heavily.

"Red, how're we looking?!" Captain Raizar called to Klay, who was in the process of removing the enormous chains. "Almost got it!" he replied as he strained with the large object. "There!" he then said as he threw off the chain. Soon enough, they had managed to clear the other chains off of the *Maiden*, leaving the anchor as the last to remove.

"It's pierced the hull; I don't think it would be smart to pull it out, could lead to more damage." Klay explained. Mason shook her head and gritted her teeth and tightly shut her eyes in frustration. "Damn...well let's at least cut its line." Captain Raizar said firmly as he moved around object and pulled at the wire that was connected to it. The fierce skirmish between the Alpha and the prisoner dragged on, and both had become increasingly tired from blood loss as it continued. Atop the ship, Captain Raizar loosed a round from his revolver that separated the line from the anchor.

"There! Got it!" Captain Raizar yelled triumphantly as the anchor's line came loose, and they all quickly scrambled off of the ship's top and around to its open ramp. He then pulled a lever on the wall near the front of the ship which opened the jaw-like doors of the hangar. As the others carried Ayb with them inside the ship, where Maelo rushed to meet them, Sonder turned and looked back at the striped prisoner, beckoning them with a call. "Come on, come with us!" The prisoner looked over at him and then quickly returned their attention to the Alpha.

In a final move, the feral escapee pinned the Albino Alpha to the crude wall of the hangar with the knife through its shoulder, causing it to screech in a high-pitched fashion as ooze-like blood trickled out from the wound. They then quickly turned and bolted towards the lowered ramp of the ship, following Sonder inside. "They're in! Close her up and get us out of here, Mas'!" hollered Klay, who had witnessed this on the rear-view screen on the ship's dashboard. Mason didn't waste a second.

In a flash, her hand instinctively found itself over the throttle and began to push it, causing the *Nameless Maiden*'s rear boosters to begin firing up as the craft started to roll forward. An increasing whine tore through the air as the ship's vapor engines ramped up, joined soon after by an electromagnetic sound, and the boosters' blinding blue glow filled the room, overtaking the blood-red flames of the chain-hung ceiling lamps.

Mason then turned her attention to the screen that depicted a live feed of what was going on behind the ship and watched as the Alpha desperately chewed and clawed at the knife that was keeping it stuck in place. Mason's eyes narrowed, and without a shred of mercy, Mason pushed the throttle as far forward as it would go. The needle on the dashboard climbed to a satisfying point, and a second, louder screech reverberated throughout the crude hangar as the they witnessed the Alpha (whose face was alight with horror) get slowly cooked and vaporized to powder by the booster engines, which then propelled the avian-shaped craft out through the opened, jaw-like doors of the scrap ship and off into the void, leaving the larger ship far behind within seconds.

Mason then took notice of the feral prisoner's hand, which had joined over hers on the throttle. She was surprised by not having noticed this a moment ago, but the feeling was overtaken by a strange sense of comradery she felt with them in the moment. Though they still appeared to be reserving their right to remain silent, they shared a look with Mason. She had a fair, humanoid face with whiskers, golden, cat-like eyes (which were dazzling up closed), and in the light of the ship's cabin, Mason could see her identity clearly. Much like with the rest of her body, she had a criss-cross of thick, black stripes on her face. The golden-eyed girl gave a slow nod before she tore away from Mason's hand and started to walk over towards the back of the cockpit-bridge.

"Hey, thanks for the save back—" Klay started to say, but the girl didn't seem to care much, if at all, for conversation, and she moved to the back of the cockpit-bridge, returning to the comfort she found in the shadows. This made Klay rub the back of his neck as he took on an understanding yet defeated look and hung his head slightly.

"Girl's been through a lot, it would seem. Most likely more than you or I could ever begin to imagine. I'd give her some space if I were you, lad." said Captain Raizar, who was just as relieved as the others to be free from the Saurossians' clutches. After finishing up the repair work on the engine, Mason managed to get the Rift Key working again, and she steered the *Nameless Maiden* out of the realm and through a rift.

. . .

From out of the rolling curtains of black mist, giant skeletal shapes appeared and closed in on the Saurossian ship.

Stage III:

A Pit Stop

"Here, for your wounds." said Jasper as he offered up gauze and tape to the striped girl, who practically tore the items from him and retreated to the darkness of the cabin in a fashion not unlike a wild beast. Jasper pulled his arms close to himself in fear as she did this. Across the room, Captain Raizar was quietly comforting Mason in her seat as Klay put the finishing touches on repairing and rebooting Ayb.

Once this was complete, the synthform's lights switched on and its metal frame rose up to standing position. "I am back online. That's much better. What has happened while my systems were out?" the robot inquired. "You got dinged up and we had to carry you the whole way back to the ship." Klay explained to him. "That's two you owe me." Sonder (who had stopped glowing) said to Ayb.

"Illogical; we are now even, mortalform." Ayb said to Sonder. The white-haired worker's face twisted up with a slight pinch of anger. "What?! No, *you* owe *me!*" he said back, but the synthform simply walked past him, saying: "That does not compute; I aided in your recruitment. You would be jobless and starving without my involvement in the previous mission." before folding back up into its box-like form as it nestled back into its socket, where it then plugged itself back into the ship.

Sonder was at a loss for words. Klay shot him a look of half sympathy. "So...*that* happened." said Sonder as he looked around at the others in the cockpit-bridge. "Yeah." added Jasper. Maelo seemed relieved to be in their company again, and the striped girl was carefully poking about the cabin, almost as if she were investigating her newly claimed territory. "So, uh, what's your name?" Sonder asked her. The girl looked over at him with those cat-like golden eyes of hers and said nothing.

"Alright, then." said Sonder. "Can she even understand us? Maybe she doesn't speak our language." he continued. Raizar gave a long "Hmm..." at this. "Speaking of which, how can I understand you guys? You say you're from a different universe, and I've seen plenty of proof of that now. But, I've still got a lot of questions." Sonder then asked the crew.

"It's pretty simple, actually. When you cross over from one realm to another, everything becomes universal. That's also why we appear similar to each other in our mind's eye, and yet,

I'm sure we all have a different perception of one another." explained Jasper, who had swiveled his chair around to face him and appeared to have been roused from his state of shock by Sonder's question. "Wow, that's...actually pretty cool." said Sonder. "Thanks for the lesson, *professor*." Klay teased. Jasper shot him a look.

"But, wait, how does that explain the other countless languages I hear in my home world? And, not to mention, Captain Raizar here has an accent. How do you explain that?" Sonder asked. "Raizar's from a different realm than yours and ours, so maybe it's just something to do with how the linguistics work out. As in, the further out you are, the more different the languages or ways of communications work. Hence why we can't understand the Saurossians. They must be from one of the really far-off realms." Jasper explained as he fidgeted with his bent-up glasses in an attempt to fix them.

Sonder, satisfied with this explanation, gave a shrug like gesture as he nodded. Their attention then returned to the striped prisoner they'd freed. "Are you sure you're comfortable over there? We have plenty of seats, you know." offered Jasper. The girl turned from where she was looking and faced him. "I'm fine where I am." she said at last, sharing her exotically-accented and fair-sounding voice with the others. As she spoke, it sounded almost as though it were being partially accompanied by a quiet, animalistic growl.

"Okay, just thought I'd offer. You know, we aren't going to hurt you." said Jasper, who outstretched his hands in a peace-offering fashion. "So, she speaks." added Klay with a sense of boredom and disinterest. Jasper shot him another look. "You're not helping." Jasper then said quietly to him. Klay just shrugged his shoulders and gave him a look that said, "*What?*" in reply. "Well, if you change your mind; seat's open." Jasper said as he gestured to the chair next to his.

Sonder then turned his attention to Mason, who looked as though she hadn't blinked for a great deal of time. Her hands were cemented to the control sticks with an iron grip. "You, uh, doing okay?" he asked her. Mason remained silent and still. "Mason?" Sonder asked. This jolted her back to reality, and she turned to slowly face him. "Sorry, it's just..." she said as she gestured about lazily. "Yeah, I know. Listen, we don't uh, we don't have to talk about what happened back there, but if you ever want to, I've got you. I'd listen." Sonder offered in response.

Mason nodded to show her appreciation of this and then turned away from Sonder as her head lowered, and her eyes seemed to drift about as they looked upon the monitors and controls before her on the dash. "Is there, uh, anything I can do to help right now?" Sonder asked. Mason shook her head slightly without looking up from the controls.

"I think it's best we just give her some space for now, man." Klay then said quietly to Sonder. Behind them, Raizar was rifling through trunks that were secured to the cabin's floor. "Ah, damn. Looks like our supply is gone." he cursed. "Oh, don't tell me..." said Klay, who dropped his head into his hands. "What? What's going on?" Sonder asked.

"They took my booze. Plus, we're out of food." Raizar answered as he turned to face the others in a dramatic fashion to say the last part. "You're kidding." said Jasper, who then mulled this over. "Those scaly bastards must've taken it all." said Raizar. "Well, it can't be helped. We'll need to make a run. Who wants to go?" he then asked the crew as he turned to face them.

"What? Are you serious? After we just survived all of *that*?" asked Klay. "No way man, I'm not going anywhere for at least a good, long while." he added. "Alright, well, when you start starving to death, don't complain to me." Raizar fired back. Klay was incredulous at this. "Excuse me?" he asked with mounting vitriol in his voice. "Last time I checked, it was your idea to run off like this. We just got dragged along with you. So, if there's anyone to complain to, I think it's you, *pal*."

This made Raizar stiffen up and as he rose, he moved closer to Klay. "You got a problem with how I run things, *Red*?" he then asked in a serious tone. "I might." said Klay, who stood to meet this challenge. The two men moved in close until they were nearly touching their chests together. Their eyes burned with anger as they stared unflinchingly at one another. The striped girl at the back of the cabin looked as though she were gearing up to break up the fight.

"That's enough." Mason said firmly, drawing everyone's attention to her. The golden-haired pilot had turned around in her chair to face them. "We've been through too much together to let it all fall apart now. So, let's regroup and figure out what we're doing next." she added. At this, Klay and Raizar returned to staring each other down. "I'm gonna shelf it for now, but this ain't over, old man." Klay said with venom in his voice. Raizar just nodded as he stood in place. "Now, I have a few ideas of where we might find some emergency supplies nice and easy. After all, we don't exactly have a lot to barter with." Mason then explained.

"What do you have in mind?" Klay asked after walking over to her and peering over her shoulder. "Well, let's see." Mason said as she looked at the screen on her dashboard that depicted a view of the charted realms. Using her finger and thumb to grasp a small joystick, she maneuvered the cursor on the screen and clicked on one of the realm maps via the button at the stick's top. This brought the view on the screen closer to the mapped region and gave examples of the charted worlds they could visit. "Ayb, could you help me punch up ideas? We're looking to pick up some grub." Mason asked the repaired synthform.

"Certainly, Ms. Vohldt. Collating data for 'mortalform sustenance.'" the mechanical being said in response as his program began to search for options, something that gave off a quiet clicking sound as the strip-lighting on his chassis flickered.

"What about over there, on Sphere 9?" Klay asked. "No, no. We hit them last week, no way they'd let us get away with it again." answered Mason. "Sphere 10, maybe?" "No." "Sphere 11?" "Okay, now you're just counting up." "What? I'm hungry; can't help it." Sonder felt like asking another question at this. "Why do you guys go by a simple numbering system? I've been wondering about that." Mason and Klay turned to him and Jasper answered almost straight away for them both. "Well, when you're charting the multiverse with a threat like we're dealing with hot on your tail, you don't exactly have the sort of time needed to come up with any interesting names. It's the same with realm designations. Just makes it all simpler, I suppose. Granted, a civilization may have a name in mind, of course, and we update it to be more accurate in the database. But, that's only if our meetings with them go over well."

"Do they not normally go well?" Sonder asked. "Well...no. Not really. We've tried everything; lying, stretching the truth, and just straight-up telling people. But, usually, it doesn't go the way we think it will, and we end up either running for our lives or getting involved in something we shouldn't have." Jasper answered and explained. "Huh. Makes sense, I guess." said Sonder, reflecting on all of this. "Oh! Here we go. Ayb found something good. Sphere 3-46. It hasn't been visited by the network in any way yet and it's only advanced as far as internet and cellular communication." Mason piped up. "Sounds good to me. Should be a quick, easy, in-and-out procedure." added Klay. With this, they had their destination and moved over to it aboard the *Nameless Maiden*, traveling through another rift.

On the other side was a planetoid that had a deep-blue coloration to it and its background was a void full of twinkling lights. Land masses of varying sizes filled in the spaces between the water, and though one of its asymmetrical hemispheres was engulfed in darkness, this was remedied by thousands of little lights coming from cities that were spread out over its surface. A blazing, white star creeped ever-so-slightly out from behind it.

"Wow, that looks a lot like home." said Sonder, who was still dazzled by the sights of space travel. "Yeah, it's very similar. But, 3-46 isn't quite as advanced as your home world. We should be able to drop in, get some food supplies, and get back out without any push-back." said Mason. She then turned to the others and said: "Alright, now I want a clean run, no messes like last time, okay?" Sonder knew she was referring to the run involving his "recruitment," for lack of a better term.

"Right." said Klay, who gave Sonder another sympathetic look. Mason then landed the ship, which came to a rolling stop outside a small gas station attached to a convenience store. As the crew of the *Nameless Maiden* walked down its loading ramp and were met with a cool rush of air and a view of the planet's evening sky, Sonder asked:

"Are you sure this is a good idea? I mean, it doesn't look like these people even have space travel yet. We might be causing more trouble than you guys realize just by being here." "Relax, quit your whining; we need food." countered Klay as he took a hit from his pen and released a large plume of white vapor into the open air. The growing sense of hunger in Sonder was enough for him to shrug off his concerns and continue following Klay, Mason, and Jasper down the ramp. The striped girl tailed them but remained by the ship once they had moved far enough away.

"You're not going with them?" Raizar asked, startling the girl with his sudden appearance. He was sitting at the top of the ship's ramp and lighting up a smoke with a metal flick-lid lighter. "I'm staying right here." she answered firmly. "Suit yourself." said Raizar, who took a long drag off of his cigarette. A black cloud escaped his lips as he exhaled moments later. The girl didn't seem to be bothered by Raizar's company, so he decided to continue talking. "I take it you're fine with staying with us for the time being?" he asked the striped girl, who nodded at this.

"Alright. We'll have to clear out some space for you in one of the rooms, but this shouldn't be a problem." Raizar said. Then, there was a short period of silence. The smoking captain broke this by saying: "You know, I think spending some time with the others might do you some good." he said. The girl said nothing. "You're only going to be young for so long, and with a lifestyle like ours? There's always a chance you'll lose people. After all, Sonder's the one who helped you get out. Couldn't hurt to get to know him." Raizar continued.

"Don't remind me." She said with a slight growl in her voice. It seemed like Raizar had touched a nerve. "Why's that?" he ventured, looking over and down at her as she leaned against the frame of the *Maiden*. "The tribe I hail from does not tolerate weakness. It's part of why I'm in this mess to begin with." The girl explained. "I've got a life-debt to pay back now, and it's not an easy thing to live with if you're someone like me." she continued.

"Oh, I see." Raizar said in response. "Well, it still stands; I think you should join them. But, I won't force you. It's your life, after all." This got the girl to look up at him with a look of hope in her golden eyes. Raizar met them with his and gave her an encouraging smirk. Then, with a remote, he cued on his favorite selection of soothing country music, which rang out of the speakers inside the open ship.

The others pushed open the glass door of the convenience center, causing its bell to jingle, and were greeted with a lazy and aloof "Welcome in." by the clerk, who was standing behind a counter with registers on it. She was dressed in a shirt with the gas station's logo on it and a pair of jeans. It looked as it were several hours into her shift, based on her sloth-like demeanor. Playing quietly over the intercom system that ran throughout the store was a muffled reggae-style song. As Sonder and the others walked through the short aisles lined with various food items and candy, they talked with one another.

"I just realized, are we just bringing that girl along with us, or?" Jasper asked Klay. "That's another Ozo decision. If she ends up staying, though, it means another mouth to feed." Klay complained. "Hey!" Jasper said with a scowl before lightly hitting Klay on the arm. "What?" "You're always such a butt about these things." Sonder asked Mason as they followed behind the other two:

"So how old are you guys anyways? I've been meaning to ask." "Oh, good question. Klay's about twenty-five, and Jasper's twenty-one. No one knows exactly how old Ozo is, but I'd say he's probably around forty. It's also your best guess how old Ayb is." she answered. Sonder chuckled at this. "Wait, so how old are you?" he then asked.

The girl stopped and turned to him with a playful look on her face.

There was a sense of daring and adventure in her deep blue eyes. "Guess." Sonder knew he had to be careful here. Thinking for a moment, he took a stab at guessing. "I'm gonna say twenty." he said with uncertainty. This got a few giggles out of Mason. "Aww, you're cute." she teased. "Well?" Sonder asked. "I'm twenty-four." the girl answered. Sonder was slightly shocked to hear this. She looked as though she was fresh out of college, to his estimations at least.

He wondered if they had colleges where she and the others had come from. "How 'bout you?" "Oh me? I think I'm twenty-two." Sonder answered. "You think? Aww, little baby." Mason teased him in a similar voice to a parent talking to a newborn. "*Stoooooop.*" Sonder said in response with a grin on his face. The group continued to peruse the shelves, occasionally making a selection or two of chips and candy. Meanwhile, the clerk behind the register had begun to question the starship parked outside.

"So where exactly are your families?" Sonder then asked. He wondered where their parents must be with them being as young as they are. "Oh, my uh...my parents are gone." explained Mason, whose mood dropped slightly at this. "Oh, I'm sorry for your loss." "No, no, it's not like that. They're just missing. They actually joined up with the resistance before I did." "Oh. Okay." "Yeah. I'm holding out hope, though. They'll turn up eventually. They always do." Mason said with a sense of hopefulness. "What happens if they find out about you deserting the cause?" "Well, that's actually part of the reason I walked out with Raizar and the others. The network wouldn't use up resources trying to find them, especially since they could be anywhere in the multiverse."

"Hmm. I guess that's true. I hope you find them soon." "Thanks. But, I'm actually hoping *they'll* find *us*. Until then, I'm just going to keep moving. My grandfather is actually still stationed with the resistance somewhere, and he's not exactly thrilled that I left." "Oh, man." "Yeah, I tried to get him to come with us, but he's very loyal to them." "He really picked the network over you?" "Yeah." "That's...gotta be rough."

"Well, it's become par for the course at this point for me. Things are rough all around." Sonder couldn't help but feel bad for her after hearing this. "As for the boys; Klay and Jasper are orphans who lived on the streets together. Ozo and I and gave them a home during one of our runs." "Wow. That's really kind of you guys." "I'm glad to have them with us. When it was just me and Raizar, things were tough. It was difficult when a synthform was the only tie-breaker."

"How is Jasper so smart, though? Was he educated before getting orphaned?" "He reads a lot. Used to borrow books from the library in their home town. Klay's a total meathead, so he's always been like Jasper's bodyguard." As Mason said this, Klay turned and gave Mason a look that made her chuckle.

"So, how did you meet Ayb and Captain Raizar?" Sonder asked. "Funny story; he actually tried to steal my ship with Ayb's help." "Wait, really?" Mason laughed at this. "Yeah, luckily it has an emergency override on the fob." she explained as she held out the ship's key ring, which had a small box with buttons on it. "After apologizing profusely and offering to clean it top-to-bottom in exchange for me piloting it for him and joining the cause, we got along just fine." Mason explained.

This made Sonder burst into laughter. "That's great." he then said. "So, uh, which universe—er, realm, are you guys from?" Sonder then asked Mason. "Oh, good question. I'm from 7. Raizar hasn't told us where he's from, but my best guess is that he's from a far corner of 5. The boys are from 8, which is actually about a stone's throw away from your world." she answered.

"What do you mean? Are the realms like right next to each other, or?" "Oh, no, silly. They're technically all existing around the same place at the same time, kind of like a big stack of pancakes." "Huh. Neat." Sonder had started to come to terms with this reality and was growing more comfortable with it. He was now also very hungry for pancakes. "Those sound good right about now..." he said aloud.

"Oh, I think they've got some over in that aisle." Mason said as she directed him to the microwave breakfast selection. Though it wasn't exactly his first choice, it was certainly better than nothing. After grabbing a couple boxes, he returned to the others. "You guys have a microwave, right?" Sonder asked Mason. "Yeah, of course." she answered. "Do you guys cook on the ship?" Sonder then asked her. "We used to, but there hasn't really been a lot of time for stuff like that. At least, not since we started doing runs, that is." Mason explained. Sonder nodded.

"I suppose we probably should, but, we all kind of suck at cooking, to be honest." Mason then said while laughing slightly. By now, the clerk had picked up the phone and made a call about the spaceship she saw outside. "Well, actually, Ozo used to cook for us, but, that was before..." Mason trailed off. "Before what?" Sonder asked. Mason stopped dead in her tracks and turned around slowly with a look of unease on her face. "Whoa, I mean, if I'm prying too much, stop me." he then said as he held up his hands in a defensive, peace-making gesture.

"It's okay, it's just...well, I'm not sure he'd want me talking about it." said Mason. Back outside, Raizar had already smoked down most of the cigarette. He and the striped girl were looking up at the stars and enjoying the nice breeze. "So...this is another realm." said the striped girl, as though none of this was particularly surprising to her. "Yeah, that's right." Raizar said as he looked down at her with an impressed look. "How did you know that?" he then asked her. She took a moment before answering. "My clan was gifted something from an outside visitor that allowed them to travel between realms. Most left our home in search of other battles. I stayed behind with a small group of the clan; we believed we could still turn the tide somehow." she explained. Her head lowered as she stated this last part. "My condolences. I'm sorry to hear that." Raizar said in reply. A long moment of silence filled the air.

"Got a name?" Raizar then asked her. "Why do you care?" she bit back and shot him a fierce look with her golden, cat-like eyes. "Touchy." Raizar remarked under his breath. "Well, since it seems like you're stuck with us for the time being, it might help to have a name to go with your face." Raizar then said. The striped girl thought this over for a moment and then ultimately decided to take the leap.

"*Orfa.*" she said simply. "I am Orfa of the Yarggen Clan." "Ah, well met, Orfa. I'm Captain Ozomatli Raizar, at your service." he said as he extended his hand down to her. She didn't shake it. This was either due to her not knowing the custom or her reserved nature. Raizar cleared his throat as he retracted his arm and returned to the comfortable sitting position he had been in. It was then that Maelo came out and joined them. "Oh, Maelo, my boy!" Raizar said joyously as he threw his hands up before bringing them back down and petting the animal vigorously. "I'm so happy you're okay. Who's a good boy? You are, yes, you are!" Raizar said as he continued petting the Vector Wolf, who only became more and more excited by this.

When he turned back to look at Orfa, he saw that she had moved closer to the ramp in order to get a better look at the dog. Her eyes were sparkling. Raizar knew exactly what she was thinking. "This is Maelo, our resident 'good boy.' Would you like to pet him?" he offered. Orfa took a second, then nodded shyly and held out her hand. Maelo walked over and sniffed the limb as his three tails started to wag happily. "He's beautiful." she said as she began petting the top of the dog's head. "You hear that, Maelo, my boy? Sounds like you have another admirer." joked Raizar, who was now smiling. Then, Maelo multiplied before their eyes into five separate dogs, surprising the girl, who was overwhelmed quickly by a flurry of licks and wagging tails. This got a big chuckle out of Raizar.

Inside the convenience store, the rest of the crew was now filling up foam cups with differently-flavored slush. Klay chose the wild red cherry one, Jasper got blue raspberry, Mason picked the green apple one, they picked out a lemon-flavored one for Orfa and orange one for the captain, and Sonder, attempting to impress them all, made a mixture of all the flavors. "Ooh, I never thought of that!" Jasper said excitedly at this. His green eyes sparkled with life. "It's all gonna blend together, though." Klay said with a slight ounce of disgust. "I think it's fun." said Mason, backing Sonder up on his idea. This made him smile broadly for the first time in practically forever.

"So, are you and Klay....?" Sonder asked Mason quietly, not wanting the others to hear. "Oh him and I? No, it's not like that. He's more like a brother to me. Just like with Jasper, and Ozo is sorta kinda the estranged father figure of our merry little group." the gold-haired pilot explained. Sonder felt a sense of relief as he heard this. "Why do you ask?" Mason then asked with a playful, accusatory look on her face.

"Oh, uh no reason." said Sonder, who tried to sweep his feelings under the rug, but his slightly flushed face gave him away. "Oh, okay." said Mason, who smiled at this and returned her attention to putting a lid on her flavored slush cup.

As they moved over towards the check-out register, Sonder decided to press once again about Captain Raizar.

"So, what happened?" he asked Mason, who wasn't exactly thrilled that he was taking up the topic again. She let out a long sigh. "He lost people. Probably the closest ones anyone could lose. It...changed him." she explained. Sonder felt bad about asking, deciding that he would restrain his curiosity going forward. "I'm sorry to hear that. I can't imagine what that must be like." Sonder said, hanging his head. Mason took on a more sympathetic face.

"You say that like you've never lost anyone." she said. Sonder stopped walking at this. "Well, that's because I have no memory of anything, really. I don't even know if I have family to begin with." he explained as he lifted his head back and looked at her with those indigo-colored eyes of his, which were a perfect window into just how lost his soul was. Mason felt a deep sense of sorrow come over her. "Come on, you guys, let's get up on outta here." said Klay, who then started to lead them to the exit door.

Sonder stopped them and said: "Wait, aren't we going to pay for this stuff?" As he looked at their confused and concerned faces, he realized. *Right.* Then, he led them over to the check-out register and placed the microwave pancakes and other frozen meals, bags of chips, chocolate candies, and his slush drink on the counter in front of the clerk, who was doing her best to act normal under these circumstances.

Sonder then gestured for the others to do the same. A thought then came over him as he felt around in his empty pockets. *Wait, what are we going to pay with?* He felt a growing sense of panic come over him as the nervous clerk rang up the items with the price gun. Each time its laser encountered a barcode, the device made a loud and quick *BEEP!* and the employee moved the item over before moving on to the next. As the pile of yet-to-be scanned objects shrank, Sonder's mind began to race with ideas. Then, Klay broke the tension. "So, Sonder, what are you going to pay with?" he asked the white-haired boy, almost in a teasing fashion, like the whole idea of paying was silly.

Sonder's blood went ice-cold as the clerk's body stiffened up and locked eyes with him. "Uhhh...." Sonder said aloud. "Here, with this." said Jasper, who stepped forward and offered up a blue, gem-like object that glistened in the light. "Should be more than enough to cover it." "Wait, what is it?" Sonder asked him. "A universal commodity, let's just put it that way. You could probably buy this establishment and every other chain in existence with it." Jasper explained. The clerk behind the register's eyes widened as she heard this and took the gem from Jasper with a slow, shaky grasp.

"Are you serious? You just had one of those in your back pocket?" Klay asked the boy, who gave a shrug in reply. He then perked up as he realized what else he had in his pocket, something the others didn't notice. "Does this cover everything?" Sonder asked the clerk standing behind the counter. "Uhhh...sure." she said with a nervous expression. She had really started to sweat like crazy as she witnessed all of this take place.

Taking their bagged snacks, food, and drinks into their hands, Sonder and the others then walked away from the counter and out through the entrance door, causing its bell to jingle once more as they exited the small building. Before it closed all the way, Sonder called out to the clerk and hollered: "Thank you! Sorry for the trouble!" The clerk was stunned. For a moment, she simply stood in place, completely flabbergasted by what had just happened. Then, she started to look the crystal over with curiosity.

Outside, Klay noticed a rugged and dirty-looking bearded man that was hunched down and holding a cardboard sign with big letters drawn in thick, black marker that read: *"The End is Nigh,"* which caused an uncomfortable pit to form in his stomach. Yet, there was a glistening glimmer of hope in the stranger's worn eyes as he looked upon the *Nameless Maiden*. When they had made it back to the ship, Sonder and the crew noticed an approaching mass of flashing red and blue lights from far off down the road, and a collective wailing of sirens could be heard drawing closer.

"That's our cue." said Klay with a rising urgency in his voice. Mason picked up her pace and led the others quickly up the ramp of her ship before closing it up behind them. Moments later, she switched on the engines and steered the vehicle onto the road next to the gas station. It then began to roll forward as it picked up speed. Soon enough, it lifted up and away into the air and then breached the upper atmosphere of the planet, leaving it in the dust as it ventured through another rift.

Now that they were back aboard the ship with their snacks in tow, the crew nestled into their seats inside the cockpit-bridge and pigged out. Mason turned to Sonder and smiled before saying: "Thank you, by the way." "For what?" he asked her in response. "For asking all those questions. You helped keep my mind busy after everything that just happened. Plus, thinking about all of the good stuff brought my mood up. So, thank you." Sonder returned this with a smile.

Suddenly, a realization came over Jasper and he decided to bring up what he had found earlier. "Oh shoot, that's right!" he suddenly exclaimed as he drew out the small tablet from his pocket. As his eyes lifted back up, they met the confused faces of the crew around him. "Uh, sorry. Let me explain: back when we got captured, I found this little guy in one of the rooms the Saurossians were using to store stuff in. I'm not sure if this belonged to a victim or if it was just something they'd found while out scavenging the realms, but it looks to be a map of '13' that shows where to find *Geleur* artifacts." he then explained.

"How did you only remember this now?" asked Klay. "Well, to be fair, we were all still recovering from our last little adventure. I wasn't exactly sure when a good time to spring this would be." answered Jasper. Klay made a shrug of agreement at this. "Gell-e-yur...what?" Sonder asked. "Ancient, advanced travelers from another world that seemed to have been doing this whole rift game for a lot longer than we have. They disappeared some years ago, though. Not entirely sure why. But! This tablet has a complete chart of 13, including where they stashed their good stuff." Jasper explained.

"How has that thing not run out of power by now?" Klay asked him. "Beats me, maybe the Geleur figured out the whole 'infinitely-sourced energy' thing." Jasper answered. This got a pensive "Hmm..." out of Klay, as if it were potentially dubious. Suddenly, Sonder felt as though destiny was calling out to both him and the crew. "Guys, I think we should use it." he said to them. "And do what with it?" Klay asked, sounding pessimistic as usual.

"I don't know, to go out and hunt for anything that could be useful. Something tells me that we were meant to find this thing, just like how I feel that you guys were meant to find me and..." he looked over at the striped girl. "Orfa." she finished for him after finishing a bag of 'Flaming-Hot' chips. Sonder gave her an appreciative smile at this.

"Also, isn't it part of your mandate to seek something like this out?" suggested Sonder. Jasper was in agreement with him. "This could really help everyone out, Klay. Maybe it is time to return to the fight." he said, backing Sonder up. "That's Ozo's decision." Klay said firmly, drawing a sigh out of Jasper.

"No, Jasper's right." Mason piped up and said. "We've been sitting everything out for too long, and I'm tired of running." she added. Sonder looked inspired by this and was glad to have suggested the idea. Jasper felt a sense of hope growing within him. "Then it's settled." Captain

Raizar said as he stepped inside the cockpit-bridge cabin. "We'll go." he added as he straightened the hat on his head and gave an encouraging smirk.

Stage IV:

The Knell

*T*he *Nameless Maiden* re-entered Realm 13

through a rift, which closed up behind it, and it
rocketed through the black mist and towards one
of the floating plateaus that was nestled inside the
would-be protective bounds of its covered-up
crystalline palisade. Above the small, upside-down
mountain-like world was one of the smaller gems,
which was covered up with the blackened sinew
they'd seen before. Sonder started to glow once
again.

"I don't like this..." said Klay. "I'm not the
biggest fan of the idea either, but, somehow it feels
right. It's like we've finally got some progress
going on. Can't say it was like that a few weeks

back, now can we?" asked Mason, countering Klay's nerves. "Either way, let's try our best to make this as smooth of a run as possible, okay? I don't want to be out here for too long. This place gives me the creeps" said the rusty-red-haired man.

As they drew closer to the floating, mystical-looking world, they could see with limited visibility that there was a large, temple-like structure covering most of its middle portion. It was surrounded on all sides by a reddish-orange sand that was completely still, as if the weather on the plateau had ceased and it was frozen in time. For Sonder, something was strangely familiar about it. "Jasper, what's the map say about this place?" Sonder then asked the bespectacled young man, who looked over the alien tablet.

"According to its charts, and Ayb's loose translating, it appears to be a world called

'Mythoss.' Unlike planets, which feature a variety of biomes and climates, these...*plateaus*, if you will, are home exclusively to one type of environment and appear to have been designed for a single purpose by the hands that shaped it. The inverted mountain underneath it is chock-full of naturally-occurring resources. This world, Mythoss, is home to a temple that contains a plethora of Geleur artifacts, which means—" Jasper blathered on.

"Short version, please." Klay interjected as he rolled his eyes and then looked over at Jasper with an impatient expression. They were, after all, against the clock when venturing into this realm. "Fine; cool little world with a temple that has fun, useful things in it. Better?" Jasper asked him in a slightly snarky tone. "Better." said Klay, unbothered by this.

"Right, so we go down, scope it out, and see what we can find." said Sonder. "Quick and easy in, quick and easy out. I like it. Let's get moving." added Raizar. With this, Mason steered the *Nameless Maiden* past the giant, covered-up crystal that hung above the world in the sky, and down towards the plateau's surface. "I'm not picking up any mortalform signals. The plateau appears to be safe." said Ayb. The ship kicked up reddish sand as it touched down and rolled to a stop. Its floodlights illuminated the immediate area.

"Is it even safe to go out there? I mean, without suits and all." Sonder inquired. "Oh, that's the fun of 13; it's mostly breathable. Outside temperature looks to be safe, too." explained Mason, who indicated the readings on one of her screens. "The black mist between the worlds is actually oxygenated, believe it or not." she continued. Once it was safe to do so, the shore party, consisting of Klay, Ayb, Raizar, and Sonder, disembarked from the ship and approached the gloomy, sandstone brick temple. Orfa stayed behind to guard Mason, Jasper, Maelo, and the ship.

"I'll be here on comms if you boys need me. Holler if you run into any trouble. I can also send Maelo out if you need help carrying stuff." Mason explained to them on their wrist-worn comms devices. Sonder had been given one of these as well. "Not this time; the dog is staying on the ship. I don't want him running loose in a place like this." Raizar spoke into his comms device.

On the other end of the line, he could hear Maelo whine at this. Walking over to it, the darkened structure loomed high above their heads. Its size was imposing up close. "Well, this looks like an inviting place if I've ever seen one." said Klay. Thinking to enter through what they perceived to be the main entrance (an absurdly enormous, sheer stone door lined with runic patterns), the shore party approached it and searched it all over for a way to open it. Ayb had switched on a pair of shoulder-mounted lamps to help with visibility. Though there was still some residual light coming off of the smothered crystal above (which cast the plateau in an eerie glow) the surface of the plateau beneath it was incredibly difficult to make out.

"Did Jasper happen to mention a way inside?" asked Captain Raizar. "Would you like me to cut it open, Captain?" asked Ayb the synthform. "By all means, go ahead and give it a try, my friend." said Raizar as he gestured to the door before them. The synthform then rose up to its maximum height as a panel opened up on his front, exposing the barrel of a gun-like object that became red-hot within seconds.

Then, a wire-thin, red laser beam fired out at the door and left black burn marks as the synthform turned slowly from left to right. Sonder, Klay, and Raizar had to shield their eyes from the beam's intensity, and they backed away from the growing heat of it. Chips of rocks and powder blew away as the laser seared into the stone door at an incredibly slow rate. They would be there for ages if they let this go on. "Ayb, is there any way to speed this up?" asked Captain Raizar. "I am working as quickly as I can, Captain." explained the synthform. "We don't have time for this." said Klay, who shook his head at this. "Ayb, cut the laser." Raizar ordered, and the synthform shut off the function and closed the panel on his front back up.

Then, as Sonder stepped towards the stone door, he felt a sort of resonating effect deep within him, and the glow of his skin intensified the closer he got to it. "Huh. Weird." He reached out his hand and placed it on the smooth surface of the stone door. As he did this, the runes on the door began to take on a bright white coloration, matching that of Sonder's skin. "Whoa..." Raizar remarked as his eyes became wide with wonder. Klay, too, stared in amazement at this. Then, the door shifted and dust shook away from it as it began to rise up, revealing pitch-darkness inside. A decrepit-smelling, warm blast of air issued forth from the mouth of the entrance, causing the shore party (save for Ayb) to cover their mouths as their clothes were shaken about by it.

"Man, something *died* in there." remarked Sonder. "Yeah, that's what I'm afraid of." added Raizar as he led them inside with a slow step and drew out his revolver. Klay drew one of his guns also, and Ayb configured himself for potential combat, with the panels on his wrists and shoulders opening up to reveal gun barrels and the sawblade from before. "Well, whatever this temple is hiding, we'd better find it quick. I feel like we've already been here for too long." said Klay. "Don't worry, we'll be in-and-out." Captain Raizar said to the rusty-red-haired man in a reassuring tone. "Just remember, if you happen upon a living shadow, *don't let it touch you.*" he then cautioned. Sonder was puzzled by this, but let it go for the time being.

As they entered into the darkness of the temple, which Ayb cut through with his lamps, the shore party saw that the interior was made up entirely of claustrophobic stone walls and ceilings. Hung on the walls were empty, evenly spaced out slots for torches. The temple's floor was covered with sand of a white coloration that had foot-sized imprints in it that made everyone uneasy.

"I don't like this." said Klay. "You can go back to the ship, you know." countered Raizar, who gave him a look of encouragement. Klay sighed at this. Continuing inside, they noticed an archway leading to another hall to their right, and another to their left some distance in. "Which way should we go first?" Sonder asked. Captain Raizar gave this some thought for a moment before deciding. "I say we keep going straight; see where the main hall takes us. When we reach the end, we'll split into two paired groups." he said with firm gusto. And so, they kept on walking down the hall for some time.

"Ayb, are your sensors picking anything up?" the captain then asked the synthform, who responded with: "Nothing, Captain. It appears this temple may have already been picked clean by others." Ayb answered and explained. "Hmm. Well, let's stay on our toes, just in case." After reaching the end of the main hall (which felt to them like it was miles long), they split up into pairs like Raizar had said earlier.

"Red, Snow, you go that way. Me and Ayb will check out this one to the right. Here, take one of Ayb's lamps." ordered Raizar as he retrieved and handed over the light to Sonder and Klay, who nodded to show acknowledgment of this before turning and heading down the hall to their left. The darkness of the halls smothered them like a dense blanket. It was almost suffocating. Sonder began to wonder what the purpose of such a temple was. Even though he was accompanied by Klay, Sonder couldn't help the growing sense of isolation that was coming over him.

"How are you holding up, Klay?" Sonder decided to ask the rusty-red-haired man as they continued walking. "I hate this." he answered. Sonder gave him a sympathetic look at this. "I'll be better once we're back on the ship, don't worry. This trip better be worth it, though." he continued. "I hope so, too." Sonder added.

Soon enough, they happened upon the first room of the hall—an evenly spaced cube that the pair investigated cautiously. After stepping inside, they could see that there were what appeared to be carved inlets in the stone walls that looked as though they once housed weaponry of some kind that was similar to the ones humans used. Deeming it empty, they moved on to another room that was further down the hall, which yielded identical findings. "Looks like someone beat us to the punch, this place has been picked clean." said Sonder. Klay was not happy.

After searching through the rest of the rooms in the hall and finding nothing, they continued on until they came upon another sealed door that had a different runic patterning to the one found on the temple's front entrance. "Sonder, work your magic." Klay said, gesturing to the door. At this, Sonder approached it and placed one of his glowing hands on the door.

But, instead of opening, the door began to absorb Sonder, pulling him into it. "Help! Help!" cried Sonder, and Klay scrambled to quickly grab ahold of him, but the effort was wasted as Sonder was slowly ripped away. "Sonder! Sonder!" Klay yelled as he was powerless to save his companion, only being able to witness what was happening to him. Soon enough, Sonder had completely disappeared through the door, leaving Klay alone in the dark hall.

Instinctively thinking fast, Klay lifted the comms device to his face and yelled into it: "Ozo! Ozo, come in!" "What's going on?" asked Captain Raizar. "We found a door and it...well, it *ate* Sonder!" Klay explained. "What?!" Raizar exclaimed. "Yeah, I don't know man, this place is really starting to freak me out!" yelled Klay. "Stay where you are, we're coming to you!" said Raizar.

Left to his own devices, Klay was overcome with a profound sense of panic and fear. *If he's dead, this is all completely my fault.* He thought to himself, thinking back to how this had all started. On the other side of the door, Sonder fell onto his behind and let out a loud "Oomph!" as this happened. Being that Klay was the one with the lamp, Sonder could see nothing in the pitch-darkness. "Great." he said quietly to himself as he got up and rubbed his backside. He then lifted the comms device up to his face and switched it on before speaking into it.

"Hey, uh, guys? Can you hear me? I made it through the door. There's a big room on the other side." The only reply was static. He decided to try again, just in case. "Anyone read me? This is Sonder, over." Again, there was nothing but static.

"Damn it." Sonder cursed. Though he was completely unsure of how exactly he should proceed, Sonder decided that it would still be best to check out the room. Still, he had to overcome the pit of fear forming in his stomach. He felt like a small, helpless child in a world of pure darkness.

Finding his courage, Sonder steeled himself, took a deep breath, and stepped forward into the room. Clearly, something had wanted him here. "Alright then, show me what I'm here for." Sonder said aloud, as if addressing the temple itself. It was then that he noticed it—a tiny, glimmering sparkle at the far end of the room. Feeling drawn to it, Sonder walked slowly over to it and found that it belonged to a blue gem that was set into some sort of sword hilt.

As he approached it, the glow he was giving off intensified, illuminating the entire room. Sonder could see that next to the sword in the wall were dozens of other blade-sized holes, likely belonging to other weapons which were now missing. He felt a strange sense of belonging as he drew closer to the object, which was embedded into a wall lined with decorative runes which appeared to reflect Sonder's glow. Reaching out slowly, Sonder took the handle of the weapon into his hand and pulled on it. As he drew it from the wall, he was somewhat disappointed to find that the length of the sword was actually far shorter than he had been led to imagine. Instead, it was much more like a dagger.

"Aw, man..." he found himself saying aloud as he looked over the gem-imbued dagger in his hands. The gem's glow reached a critical point before dimming back down. Then, it glowed bright once more before dimming again. The repeated pattern was not unlike a slow heartbeat. "Huh. Weird." Sonder remarked. He then noticed that the runic patterning on the wall started to twist about and contort into different shapes. When they had settled, Sonder's eyes widened as they looked upon what seemed to him like some sort of prophecy being depicted.

There were three figures of light (made up of the radiating blue-white energy) and behind this was a demonic-looking dragon (which was being created by the negative space between the lighting). The three were standing on some sort of pedestal of stairs. Crowds of people were knelt down before them at the base of the stairs, indicating that these were likely powerful beings worthy of worship. The numerous slots for the knife-like weapons were within their cores, with the centermost one being the one that Sonder had drawn out from the one he was holding. "Whoa..." Sonder said aloud as he looked upon the mural of lights.

Suddenly, his comms device crackled to life, and he heard Mason's voice as she spoke. "—need to—!" she yelled, her words sounding incoherent due to interference. Lifting the device to his face, Sonder replied to this with: "Say again? Come in, over!" More static filled the line. "This is Sonder, come in, please!" he urged over the voice channel. "Sonder?! Oh, thank goodness!" answered Mason. "Yeah, I'm here, what's going on?" Sonder asked her. "You need to get out of there right now!" she yelled with dire urgency. "Wait, why? What's going on?!" Sonder asked the pilot.

"They're here! The forces we've been running away from; they've found us!" explained Mason, her voice sounding somewhat regretful, as if she wished they had told Sonder about the truth of their pursuers earlier. Before he could respond, the line cut out and became filled with static once again. "Damn it!" Sonder swore. Looking to the mural on the wall once more, he could see that it had begun to dim and disappear the more he moved away from it. "Weird." he said aloud before re-centering himself and running back over to the room's entrance.

Reaching a hand tenderly outwards, he touched the door's surface and found that, this time, it didn't take him in as it did before. "Huh?!" Sonder exclaimed and then began to scramble in a panic as he slapped his hands against it repeatedly in an attempt to activate it. But, the door remained in place, and Sonder was still on the other side of it. Thinking fast, he then tried applying the knife to the surface of the wall in a few positions, but, again this failed.

Becoming frustrated, Sonder turned from the door and ran about the large, cube-like room, desperately searching for a way back out. When he found no other, he began to feel the stress in his chest reaching a boiling point. He was about to have a panic attack, something he had suffered a handful of times in his past. Fighting through the waves of fear, an idea came upon Sonder, and he thought to try it. Moving up to the mural wall, Sonder placed his hand upon it and, like the other side of the door earlier, he was pulled into it, knife in hand. When he arrived on the other side of the wall, Sonder was sure to land on his feet this time, feeling a sense of prideful accomplishment as he did this.

He also found that the dagger was giving off a source of light that was brighter than his bodily glow, helping to illuminate the darkened hall before him, which was split into three paths; one ahead, and the other two to his left and right. Instinctively, he decided to choose the one on the left and picked up into a slight jog. As he started to run, Sonder lifted the comms device up and spoke into it once more. "This is Sonder, I'm going to try and find my way out!" he explained. Yet again, static filled the line, causing him to shake his head in disappointment and frustration. "Guess I'm on my own." he then said under his breath.

Running down the halls, Sonder began to feel a sense of claustrophobia set in as it all blurred together and seemed as if he was running in circles. When he rounded one of the corners, he felt a sense of relief wash over him as he recognized the open front entrance of the temple, as he could see the *Nameless Maiden* lying in wait for him outside. The ship was illuminated by its boosters and floodlights. Charging towards the entrance, he stopped suddenly dead in his tracks and froze in place when he noticed something out of the corner of his eye to his left.

As he turned to see what it was, his blood ran cold. Standing in the doorway to the left of the exit was what looked to Sonder like a living shadow. It was clad in cloth as black as night, and upon its head was a blackened metal helmet. Its face was almost completely obscured, save for its eyes, which burned with the fires of Hell. In Sonder's mind, he could see flaming runic symbols forming to shape a name, and he heard something being repeated over and over by a chorus of dark whispers proclaiming the name of an umbral champion:

Dey-Ud-Mund...

Dey-Ud-Mund...

As Sonder stared, rooted in place, the chorus in his mind became louder, chanting the name with great intensity and reverence.

DEY-UD-MUND...

DEY-UD-MUND...

The Shade had a cruel-looking blackened sword with an orange gem set into its guard in its left hand that it raised up slowly. While the danger had been real when he was getting choked out by the Saurossian, it was nothing compared to the dread he felt in this moment. Suddenly, Sonder's glow became more vibrant, as did the dagger and the shade's sword, and he felt a strange sense of magnetism towards the shadowy man before him. But, his instincts told him to run, something he simply couldn't do, as his legs refused to move from the spot.

The Shade's blade was raised to its maximum height before being brought swiftly downwards toward the white-haired young man, who squeezed his eyes shut in the hopes that his powers—or someone—would save him in the nick of time. Instead, he felt a heavy, searing sensation as the Shade's weapon cut him from his shoulder to his waist. Sonder yelled out in pain as blood poured from out of the slash wound, soaking his worker jumpsuit. This caused him to fall to one knee and clutch at the cut, causing blood to leak out between his fingers and drip onto the sand below him.

Thinking he should raise the dagger up in case he was about to be struck a second time, Sonder found that he didn't have the strength to, and a sense of shock and fear had completely overtaken him. Looking up, he could se the Shade winding up for another strike. Its hellish, flaming eyes were a terrifying sight from below. It was as if the evil of the world had become personified and was staring down at him. Sonder felt small in that moment. He braced for the inevitable.

Then, just before he could be struck again, Sonder heard rushing footsteps behind him, and he heard Klay yell out: "Sonder!" as the rusty-red-haired man appeared from down the hall. Klay bum-rushed the Shade, twisting his gun around to absorb the brunt of its sword swing. He pushed back against the Shade hard, causing it to backpedal a few steps. Klay then grasped Sonder by the crook of his elbow and pulled him into a run out of the temple entrance and towards the *Nameless Maiden*'s ramp.

"Come on, just keep moving! Stay with me!" encouraged Klay, who had taken notice of Sonder's state. Soon enough, they had made it to the ramp of the ship, and as Klay keyed in the sequence to close it up on the panel next to its doorway, he and Sonder stared out at the temple and watched in horror as legions of glowing-eyed humanoids poured out the temple, charging towards the parked ship. "Mason! Get us out of here!" Klay hollered on the comms device as the ramp continued to close at a snail's pace.

"Working on it!" Mason snapped back. "Where's Raizar? And Ayb?" Sonder asked Klay, sounding weak. "They're already onboard." he answered. "We thought you were dead. But, I wouldn't have been able to live with myself if I left you behind. I told Ozo and Ayb to get back to the ship and that I'd go back in and try looking for you. Damn, you're losing a lot of blood, man." Klay answered and then reacted to the wound with a look of frustration—not with Sonder, but with his situation. Sonder could tell that Klay blamed himself for all that happened to him.

"Jasper, get in here, Sonder's hurt bad!" he yelled into his wrist-worn comms device. Sonder had started to become dizzy from the blood loss, and as he began to sway from side-to-side. His glow appeared to be blinking slowly, as if threatened by his proximity to death's door.

As he looked out at the temple once more, he could see that a pair of gigantic, black, bat-like wings were stretching out at its top like claws grasping at the sky. These were soon joined by an elongated, horned reptilian head that had glowing purple eyes. The beast reared back before bellowing triumphantly into the night sky as bolts of lightning tore through the air behind it. Its scream shook the very heavens. The dragon then looked down at the ship and its eyes narrowed as its face twisted into a snarl.

"What the hell is that?!" exclaimed Klay as he, too, had taken notice of the beast atop the temple. Just before the hordes of glowing-eyed undead had reached the ship, its ramp closed right as it began to rocket forward at an alarming rate. "Hold on, boys!" Mason called to them on the comms devices. Outside, the Shade exited the temple and watched with burning eyes as the *Nameless Maiden* sped away. Inside the ramp room, Jasper and Captain Raizar stepped through the door and over to Sonder and Klay, with the medic boy quickly tending to the white-haired worker's wound. His blood had dripped all over the metal grated floor of the ship. An expression of great concern was on his face.

"What happened?" Jasper asked Klay. "He had a run in with one of the Unwilling; some kind of lieutenant, if I had to guess." explained the rusty-red-haired man. Captain Raizar looked as if he had seen a ghost when he heard this. "Sonder, are you hurt anywhere else?" Jasper then asked the white-haired young man. When he didn't answer, Jasper became frantic. "Sonder?!" he asked, but

Sonder was starting to lose consciousness. "Stay with me, damn it!" Jasper yelled. Captain Raizar was beside himself with worry. "Quick, we need to get him to the medical room!" Jasper then yelled as he started to lift Sonder up from the supply crates he had been sitting on and moved towards the door. Klay and Raizar jumped in and helped Jasper carry him.

As they did this, the dagger slipped from out of Sonder's grip, clattering to the floor of the ramp room and catching everyone else's attention. The weapon and its gem quickly lost their glow. "What's this?" Captain Raizar asked as he looked over at it. "Beats me, Sonder must've found it in the room he got sucked into." Klay explained.

"Guys, hurry!" Jasper urged the two of them, and they all moved Sonder quickly inside the ship's hallway and then into the medical room, placing him onto the table in the center of it.

Under the lights, Sonder was becoming more and more pale due to the amount of blood he was losing. Jasper then swung an arm of the medical system over the table and activated it. Within seconds, the computer connected to it registered the type of wound Sonder had suffered and how to properly stitch it up and bandage it. Jasper then keyed in the necessary sequence of buttons for it to do this, and gave a motion of his hands for everyone to stand back from the table, allowing the medical system to go to work.

It was then that Orfa and Maelo entered the room and looked upon Sonder, a sight that made the vector wolf whine and the striped girl become distraught. Sonder's eyes looked loosely around the ceiling of the room, and he appeared to be losing a sense of awareness, as he wasn't visibly registering the presences of anyone else in the room. "Sonder?" Jasper called to him again, but his eyes appeared to be getting heavy, and his eyelids started to close. "Sonder?!" cried Jasper. But, no response came from the wounded man.

"Damn it..." Klay cursed under his breath as he lifted his arms up over his head. Captain Raizar turned around and shook his head in a defeated manner. Then, he stormed off through the door and returned to the ramp room, retrieving the dagger from the floor before looking it over. "All that, just for this?" he asked himself quietly. Maelo had come up behind him and continued to whine.

Back inside the cockpit-bridge, Mason looked up through the windshield to witness the ribcage-like ships appearing above the plateau and countless undead dropping down from them and onto the ship, landing hard with a loud *THUD!* "Damn it!" the pilot cursed at this. "Guys! We've got a big problem!" she called out to the others on the comms channel. "Captain?!" Klay rushed out of the medical room and called to Raizar. "*Blondie*, can you shake them off?" the captain called to her over the comms channel on his wrist.

"I can't take off with all this added weight!" she answered. "Damn. Alright then. Klay, Orfa, you're with me!" Raizar then ordered as he ran over to the middle of the ship's hallway and reached up to press a sequence of buttons in on an access panel in the ceiling. A moment later, a long panel (set between the fluorescent lights) slid away to reveal a ladder that swung down and locked into place on the floor. Then, the ship's top hatch opened up, and Raizar started up it with the dagger in hand.

"What exactly are you going to do with that?!" Klay asked, calling out to the captain. "I'm improvising! I have a feeling this weapon might hold an important secret." Raizar explained, pausing his climb as he did so. "Like what?!" Klay asked. "It's a *knell*." said Raizar. Klay was baffled, but guessed that the captain must know what he was talking about and decided to follow him up. Orfa came up right behind him.

When they reached the top of the ship, they were greeted with the harrowing sight of undead men with glowing eyes that were rapidly approaching them. Their feet were being secured to the ship's hull by a strange, black, web-like shadow that appeared to be coming out of them. The Unwilling were wielding clubs and swords.

Thinking quickly, they copied this by clamping the cargo straps to themselves. The ship shook beneath their footing as it sped across the sandy surface of the plateau, and the wind roared as it blasted past them. With the *knell* in hand, Captain Raizar pulled himself into a defensive stance and pointed the dagger's blade outward, towards the zombie-men, who almost looked offended in a sense by the weapon's presence. Then, without any kind of warning, the front most Unwilling let out a screech before leaping at Raizar. Klay's heart felt as though it had stopped.

Adjusting his stance like a professional fencer, Raizar guided the knell into the Unwilling's center of mass, causing it to explode into bluish dust and fall away to the wind. Klay and Orfa's eyes widened at this. They were impressed by their captain's quick-thinking and martial prowess, as well as by the magical properties of the weapon. They had never seen anything like it before.

This seemed to demoralize the rest of the Unwilling atop the ship, who then steeled their resolve and pressed forth, bum-rushing the captain. Raizar flinched as the horde charged him, but he quickly regained his composure and aimed the weapon once more. "Ozo!" Klay called out to Captain Raizar, fearful that this could be the end of him. All it would take was one of the Unwilling passing their shadow onto him and he would be finished. Likely the rest of the crew, too.

With a few decisive slashes, Raizar reduced a decent chunk of the zombies to powder before having to use the dagger to block and parry the barrage of sword-swings that the zombie-men were throwing his way. Though these were aimless and sloppy moves that could easily be countered by a trained warrior, it didn't help that there were so many of them and that they were all coming at him simultaneously.

Feeling overwhelmed, Raizar did what he could by taking out a couple more before losing his footing and falling onto his back, where he then rolled away to safety near Klay and Orfa. "Here, Red, take it!" Raizar called up to the rusty-red-haired man as he threw the dagger into his clutches. Klay nearly dropped the weapon due to how sweaty his hands had become, but his grip tightened around it and he stepped forward to confront the approaching Unwilling. He wished he had Raizar's confidence in that moment, as his legs began to quiver involuntarily as he looked upon the horde.

Holding the dagger out, Klay did the best he could, given his situation, and managed to take out a small handful of them before he fell backwards into the open hatch that was at his feet. Luckily, Orfa had seen this coming and retrieved the knell from his grasp as he fell, and she quickly undid the belt around herself before launching over the Unwilling and touching back down onto the ship's roof. She had just avoided being overtaken by the horde and drew the attention away from Raizar. The zombies were solely interested in the weapon she now held, indicated by all of them turning around and pursuing her instead of the prone Raizar, who was the far easier target.

The striped girl cut her hair with the knell, (so as to get it out of her face) before she shifted to an attacking stance and bared her fangs as she charged towards the zombies. The cut locks of long black hair blew away with the wind. With artful strokes of the weapon through the air, Orfa tore apart most of the Unwilling with the knell, revealing the last of the zombies—a massive one that was clad in heavy armor and wielded a gargantuan war hammer with both of its hands.

Orfa's eyes widened as she saw this and took an instinctive step back. Before she had time to act, the Unwilling swung its hammer into her. Only barely managing to shift her weight and the dagger around in order to absorb the shock of the attack, Orfa fell away off of the ship and sending the dagger flying into the air. At the last second, the striped girl grabbed ahold of one of the cargo belts, grasping it with a vice grip as she dangled in the rushing wind like a weed next to the *Nameless Maiden*. The war hammer-wielding zombie walked over to the edge and prepared to finish her off with the weapon, but was stopped by a sudden, bright flash of light that came from behind it that it then turned around to see.

Standing on the ship's top with the knell in his hand was Sonder, whose glow appeared to be reaching critical levels. His eyes were like lamps, and his stark-white hair was blowing upwards with the wind. As he slathered the blade of the dagger with the blood that was still on his hands (as his wound had been visibly cauterized), it suddenly became lengthened to the fullness of a sword as its runes became alight with a magic glow. He then shifted to a powerful stance. It was as if the soul of a great warrior had possessed him in that moment.

Orfa managed to get back up onto the ship's top and secured herself as she watched this, and Klay climbed back up the ladder. The pair and Raizar were completely taken by the spectacle. Sonder had become like a living star in that moment, and he launched right into action. Quickly finding the weak points in the warhammer wielder's armor, the glowing being used the short-sword-like weapon to fell his opponent in lightning-fast dashes past him.

As the Unwilling dropped to its knees, Sonder rushed over to it and sunk the blade down through its neck, causing it to explode into powder, leaving nothing but the warhammer and its armor behind, which blew away off the ship and past the crewmates. The three others looked upon Sonder with a glint of hope in their eyes. Relief washed over them all. But, they didn't even have a moment to recover. Looking up, they could see that another wave of Unwilling was dropping down onto the ship from the ribcage floating above that was slowly descending upon it.

It was as if Sonder was pure instinct; in that moment, he pulled at the knell and drew out a second one made entirely out of blindingly bright energy from the weapon itself, and he tossed it over to Raizar, who caught it and stood. Repeating this, Sonder tossed the second to Orfa and a third to Klay, and they all braced as more undead flooded onto the top of the ship and in front of them. For those wielding the copies of the knell, it was like holding a bolt of lightning in their hands.

The horde crashed against them, but before any of them could spread their shadow, they were slashed apart and turned to dust by Sonder and the others. Then, before a third wave could descend onto them, Sonder raised the main knell up into the air and concentrated all of his energy in the moment, channeling it through the blade and up at the ribcage craft, causing it and the forces it carried to burn away like paper. After this, Sonder's glow settled back down to a state of normalcy, and he looked more like his usual self. The glowing pattern on the sword disappeared as it shrank back down to being just a dagger.

They celebrated for a brief moment as the ship began to take off from the ground and into the air. "We did it!" Raizar yelled triumphantly. Orfa appeared to be proud of the others, and Klay looked relieved. "Mason, take off! We're clear!" Klay then shouted into his comms device. "On it! Get back inside, quick!" Mason urged over the comms channel as she witnessed them on one of the security feeds that showed what was going on atop the ship. She, too, had been thoroughly impressed by Sonder's abilities with the knell. With this, Mason pulled the control sticks back, causing the *Nameless Maiden* to lift off of the ground and rise into the air.

A moment later, the shadow-like dragon with glowing eyes appeared behind the *Nameless Maiden* and roared loudly, startling everyone atop the ship as it began to catch up to them. Up close, the beast's form was voracious and demented in appearance. Its scales were like rows of black, serrated fangs, and its glowing eyes were piercing to look at. Its wings were like liquid shadow as they rose and fell away, propelling the dragon towards the ship with hard strokes through the air. Another umbral name-chant could be heard in their minds as its runic name burned like wildfire behind their eyes:

Mund-Karr-Mudgeon....

This became far more intense and loud as it continued.

MUND-KARR-MUDGEON....

With this, they retreated back inside the *Nameless Maiden* and closed up the roof hatch and its ladder. They then moved swiftly into the cockpit-bridge and strapped themselves in for the flight, save for Orfa, who held on tightly to the handrail behind the chairs. The pilot then took them up into the atmosphere, where hundreds of the ribcage ships were waiting for them. She then activated the Rift Key and steered the vehicle masterfully past the ribcages and through the rift that appeared, managing to evade their grasp. Mund-Karr-

Mudgeon's jaws were about to clamp down onto the craft, but the rift closed up just in time, saving them. They were safely alone now.

"Okay...we made it...is everyone okay?" Mason asked as she caught her breath. The pilot had nearly suffered a panic attack on their way out. "Yeah, we're okay." Klay answered for everyone. "That was a little too close for comfort." said Jasper. Then, a lump-like shadow dropped from the ceiling of the cabin onto his shoulder, prompting him to start yelling.

In a flash, Orfa rushed over, retrieved the knell from Sonder and stabbed the shadow on Jasper, reducing it to powder and saving his life. She had incredible control; Jasper hadn't even been hurt by this action, as the blade of the weapon had only gone so far as to touch his skin. The boy's emerald-green eyes were wide and full of shock as he looked into Orfa's, which looked fierce up close.

Her breathing was heavy, and she was sweating immensely through the black rags she wore. As she backed away, there was a sense of hatred about her towards Jasper, as if saving his life was out of character for her. She loathed the life debt that had been placed onto her. This caused Jasper to make a sympathetic face as she backed away. Even she had to admit that she found him cute, something she kept to herself as she turned away from him. She began to see that these people might just be worth fighting for.

"Thank you." Jasper said with sincerity." Orfa simply nodded in reply. The response was somewhat cold, but Jasper could see that, buried deep within her spiky exterior was someone vulnerable and scared. It was as if she had tucked her personality away as a defense mechanism. The tension in the room settled, and everyone looked to the striped Yarggen Clan girl with appreciation and at Jasper with relief. Klay rushed over to him with his eyes wide. "Are you okay? Did it get you?" Klay started to ask in a feverish way as he looked him over. "No, I don't think so." "Are you hurt?" Klay continued his questioning. "I'm fine. Really, I'm okay." Jasper assured him. "You sure?" Klay asked, looking him directly in the eyes.

"Klay, I'm fine." Jasper said with a reassuring smile before breaking from the intense eye-contact, which made him become slightly flushed in the face. "Okay." Klay said before patting Jasper on the shoulder and stepping back awkwardly. He then lifted the small smoke pen from out of his pocket to his lips and drew in a hit. Then, he breathed out a white cloud that polluted the room with an orange-peel scent and coughed. This seemed to calm him after what they had just been through. Jasper thought to discourage Klay from this, but he didn't have the energy for it and decided to simply let it go for the time being.

"Okay, looks like we're in the clear." Mason stated as she looked over the layered, real-time map of the multiverse, which depicted tagged Unwilling ships encountered by the resistance network appearing nowhere near them. The golden-haired pilot then turned and looked at the others. Her deep-blue eyes were distraught with worry. Instinctively, she unbuckled herself and moved over towards them and pulled Jasper, Klay, and Sonder in for a hug.

"I'm glad you guys are okay." she said to them. Raizar appeared to be troubled by something and was lost in thought. Maelo was anxiously shaking to himself, prompting Jasper to move over to him and comfort him. After this, Jasper turned his attention to Sonder, who looked terribly exhausted by now. "Hey, Sonder, thanks for everything back there." he said to the white-haired worker. "Oh, uh, you're welcome." "How did you do all of that, anyway? Weren't you in critical condition just a few moments ago?" Klay asked Sonder as he started to shake the state of shock he had been in due to the overload of what happened.

"I don't know. I just felt this surge of power come over me and the next thing I knew, I was on top of the ship with the dagger in my hands after it was all over. It was like something took over from me. Or, at least, that's how it felt." Sonder explained. Everyone else looked troubled by this. "Who are you exactly?" Klay asked Sonder suddenly. "I don't know. I've honestly never known. I just found myself living the life I have one day and I've just carried on since. Anytime I try to think about it, I get these bad headaches." Sonder explained. "Hmm. Weird." said Klay. "Yeah. I don't really know who I'm supposed to be, or why I'm here." Sonder continued. The others exchanged looks of concern at this. "But, one thing is for certain: it definitely looks like you're where you need to be." said Captain Raizar. "Yeah, but why? And for what reason? Am I meant to just give into the role that's fallen into my hands and let things play out?" Sonder asked. The white haired young man's shoulders sagged, and his indigo colored eyes were full of uncertainty. "Sounds like an awful lot of work." he continued. The others couldn't help but feel bad for him. "No clue. But, I promise you this: we will help you in any way that we can. We owe you that much, at least, especially after all you've done for us in the short time we've known you." said Captain Raizar. Sonder felt encouraged by this. "Well, we're just glad you're okay." said Jasper, who looked relieved. "Yeah, seriously man, you had us scared." added Klay. Sonder smiled at this. "By the way, was there a dragon coming after us, or did I dream that up?" he then asked. "Yeah, there was. That was real." Klay answered simply. Sonder was shocked. "Wow." he said with an impressed look on his face. "So, dragons are real..." he then said to himself as he began to consider the ramifications of this. "Guess so." said Klay. "Well, we made it out in one piece. That's good. Plus, you got us something that made it worthwhile. This weapon might just be the key to turning the tide." said Jasper, who pointed at the knell, which was still in Orfa's grasp. The Yarggen Clan girl was looking over the weapon as they spoke. There was a sense of hopefulness about Jasper that Sonder hadn't seen in him before. His emerald-green eyes shone with starlight.

"Nice haircut, by the way." Klay said to Orfa, who fixed him a withering glare before turning away. "Alright, alright." Klay then muttered to himself. He was trying to break the ice in ways he knew how and was clearly not making any headway with the striped girl.

"What should we do now?" Jasper then asked the others. "I think we should show our findings to the resistance network." said Mason. "I don't think they'd want to hear from us. I mean, we're deserters, after all..." Klay said at this. "Fair point. What do you think, Ozo?" Mason said and then asked Raizar, who looked as though he had been in a deep, concentrative trance. "Captain?" Mason asked again when she got no response.

This snapped Raizar back into focus, and he turned to look at the blonde-haired pilot. "Something tells me we might be playing out a role in something manufactured." he then said. "Think it could be a trap?" Klay asked him. The captain shook his head slowly. "I don't think so. I meant that...well, we might be walking a path put into place by some sort of higher power, like the

Fates." Raizar explained, sounding far more serious than usual. Everyone in the room went silent at this, heavily considering this possibility. "Things are lining up in a way I'm not entirely comfortable with." he continued, seeming to grimace at the thought of this.

"Well, whether it is or not, we now have something that can defeat the Unwilling. I think we should use it." Jasper said firmly. Everyone else nodded in agreement. "Question is, where should we start?" asked Klay. The crew began to weigh options. Orfa piped up. "We should learn everything we can about the weapon first, including its capabilities. I have a feeling we've only scratched the surface of what is possible with it." The others were impressed and on board with her idea.

"Do we know where a lot of their forces are gathered? Maybe we could test it on them." Sonder asked Mason, who then walked back over to her control console and bent over her chair to look at the screen that had the map of the multiverse on it. After a moment of searching, Mason had an answer. "Here, look, the charted spots show that there is a large number of Unwilling on this plateau. Jasper, what's your map say about it?" she said and then asked. Jasper switched the tablet on and scrolled around on it using his fingers, quickly locating the plateau in question.

"'*Unwilling?*' So that's what you call them?" Sonder asked Mason. She and the rest of the crew went deathly silent at this. "It's...what the resistance network called them. The Guardsmen and Tech-Mages coined the term." Jasper explained. "They're all...*unwilling* subjects of a necromancer that's slowly been taking over the entirety of the multiverse. They're *undead*. Totally unkillable. Until today, of course." he continued.

"Wait, so that's what you're dealing with?" Sonder asked, sounding horrified. The crew hung their heads. "Why didn't you guys tell me sooner?" he then asked them. Still, they were silent. Then, Mason spoke. "Well, we really didn't know how you'd react to news like that. I'm sorry for keeping you in the dark for as long as we did, but we thought that it might spare you from the cruel reality we've been faced with. You know; let you live in blissful ignorance, I suppose."

"So that's what you meant...when you said my home might not be there anymore..." said Sonder, whose eyes widened as he made the realization. "Yeah. Sorry." said Klay. Another dreaded moment of silence filled the cabin. "I...understand." Sonder then said after stomaching the full weight of the revelation. In that moment, Mason wished she could have spared him the pain of knowing, but it truly was about time that he knew, something she couldn't deny.

"As...*dark*...as that may sound, we now have something that could change our reality. And it's thanks to you that we found it, Sonder." the golden-haired pilot then said. This uplifted him as well as the others. "Wait, so, are we all in on this?" Sonder asked as he looked around at everyone. "I've only just met all of you, and it's insane how all of this started, but I've made some pretty big discoveries about the world and myself since the start of this whole thing. I really do think that destiny plays a role here. Maybe I was meant to meet all of you." he went on to say. Everyone smiled as warmly as they could when they heard him say this (save for Orfa). "Yeah, I'll tag along." said Klay. "I'm in." Jasper said, his eyes practically shining. "Where you go, I go." said Orfa. "Like you even had to ask." said Mason as she crossed her arms and smirked at Sonder. "Hey, I just give the orders. You tell me where we've got to be and how, and I'll make sure we get there, my friend." added Captain Raizar. Their responses filled Sonder with warmth. With everyone on board with the idea, they proceeded with putting together a plan of action.

"Jasper, what's the tablet say?" Mason then asked the boy. "It's called *Mortiss*. Looks like some sort of...forward-operating base the Unwilling use, if I had to guess. Looks like a place where they ship in and out of. You know, to spread their shadow throughout the worlds in a calculated manner." Jasper explained. The name made everyone uncomfortable.

"Mortiss?" asked Klay. "As in, like, death? The plateau's name is 'Death?' Great. Sounds real inviting." he added. "Could also be referring to life itself. Life and death. It's kind of fitting in a way, you know?" remarked Jasper. "It's a start." said Sonder. "Wait, you've gone through everything awful we've seen lately, and yet you're gung-ho about this? What gives?" Klay asked, looking a gift horse in the mouth. "Well yeah, I mean, what other choice do we have? Fated to happen or not, things have really been lining up since we met. I'm starting to think that, maybe, I was meant to join you. Just as we might be meant to challenge the Unwilling." said Sonder. "I dunno, sounds like a load of crap to me." Klay said in response to all the 'fate' talk.

"Well, whether we like it or not, this responsibility fell into *our* laps. It's our battle to fight." said Jasper. Everyone agreed with this logic. "It might first help us to know the full potential this blade carries before we go rushing off into battle." Orfa interjected, speaking with her usual exotic accent and growl-like tone. "It would be foolish and unwise to spend such a gift like this in such a way without training ourselves first." she added.

"Agreed." said Mason, who smiled at the striped girl. "Would you be willing to show us some fighting techniques?" she then asked her. Orfa seemed almost begrudging about it all, but she had to admit that it would do everyone some good. "Sure." she answered. Everyone in the room seemed to reflect on this for a moment. They were glad to have decided on a way forward. "Wait, so we're just going to run in guns blazing without any sort of back-up?" Klay then asked. "We may have to, what with our standing in the resistance network. It wouldn't exactly be unjustified if they ignore our call." said Jasper.

"Orfa, do you think your clan could help us out?" Klay then asked her. "No. I doubt they would. In a sense, I'm not welcome in their presence. Besides, I'm not even sure where to start looking for them." the golden-eyed girl answered. "The leader of the tribe, my partner and bond, would see us as weak." she continued explaining. "Bond?" Klay asked, his interest suddenly piqued. "That must be frustrating, to not be able to go freely home to the one you love." Jasper said as he made a sympathetic face. "Yes. It is. I miss them a great deal." Orfa replied as she turned away from him.

Then, Klay turned to Raizar and asked: "You alright, boss?" "Yeah. I'll be fine. We'll go ahead with that idea. Ms. Vohldt?" he asked the golden-haired pilot. "Yes?" Mason answered. "Find a safe world for us to practice on and we'll go from there." "Yes, sir." Mason said in response before moving back over to the pilot's seat with a sense of renewed purpose in her step. "So, what exactly is it, cap? You said before that it was a 'knell.' Care to elaborate?" Klay then asked Raizar.

"Yes, it is a weapon that the Geleur and Guardsmen employed to fight Ahz-Mund. The blade is made out of the only material in the known multiverse capable of killing the Unwilling." the captain explained. "Wait, then why didn't the resistance use them?" Sonder asked. "That's because none were recovered until now." Raizar replied. "That explains a few things." Klay said after hearing this as he looked over at Sonder. "How do you know all this stuff? Seems like some kind of secret the resistance is keeping locked away from us grunts." He then continued. "That's classified, my friend." said Raizar.

"Now, if you don't mind, I'm going to lay down and rest my eyes for a bit." Raizar then explained. Klay, Jasper, and Sonder looked to him with concerned expressions. "I just...need some time to myself. Red, I'm leaving you in charge for now." he then said before turning on his heel and slowly making his way out of the cockpit-bridge room and into the hall. He then disappeared into his personal quarters as the door to the bridge slid shut. "What's up with him?" Sonder asked Jasper. "I don't know. He's been acting that way since Klay told us about your encounter back there." the young man explained. This made everyone uneasy.

"We'll have to ask him about it the next time he's up and about. But, for now, we should give him some space." said Jasper. "Alright, I found us a spot to set down on. Seats, please, everyone!" Mason called back to the others from over her chair. At this, Jasper, Klay, Sonder, and Orfa each took their seats and buckled in. Moments later, Mason had guided the ship through another rift and down onto the surface of an abandoned planet, which was made up entirely out of golden salt flats.

The *Nameless Maiden* lowered onto the midnight-streaked flats (as it was currently night-time on the hemisphere that Mason had settled on) and rolled to a stop, kicking up salty debris as it did so. "Alright, we're good to go. Orfa?" Mason said and then turned to ask the striped Yarggen Clan girl, who looked over at her. "Let's do this." Mason then said, prompting the striped girl to nod firmly before unbuckling herself and standing from the chair. She then led the others through the hallway door with Maelo in tow.

After activating the ship's parking procedures, Mason, too, stood from her seat and followed after them. As they walked past the captain's quarters, Sonder peered into the room and saw that Raizar had fallen asleep while sitting at his desk. There were dried tear streaks going down his oily face (the entire crew was incredibly grimy at this point), and in one of his gloved hands was a small, silver locket that had a bloodied picture of what looked like a woman and a young boy in it. In the other hand was a large, emptied bottle of liquor. Sonder's heart felt heavy when he saw this.

Klay patted the white-haired worker on the back and gave him a look that told him to let it go and to continue walking. Sonder shook it off and did as Klay was urging him to do. The crew then poured out of the *Nameless Maiden*, walking down its ramp and onto the floodlight-lit salt flats with the knell in-hand. "Right, so, where do we start?" Mason asked Orfa. "Let's take it from the top. This is how you *hold* the weapon..." the striped girl began with a somewhat dry but entirely serious tone of voice as Mason switched-on a hip-hop track on a boom box she had brought down with them.

. . .

After an entire night of exploring how exactly the weapon worked and discovering numerous surprising ways to wield it, the confident crew went back up inside the Nameless Maiden to rest up as the light of a star creeped up over the mountains of salt in the far distance. They all had a big day ahead of them.

Stage V:

The Battle of Mortiss

"Remember, now, just as we practiced, my *Vector Wolves*!" "We?!" Sonder turned to Captain Raizar and asked, having to yell slightly over the sound of rushing wind. Staring out from the lowered ramp were Sonder, Raizar, Orfa, Klay, and Ayb. They had tightened themselves into their battle-ready stances and were preparing to jump down into the flare-lit chaos. "It'll be fine!" Raizar shouted back. "Here we go." Sonder said to himself, readying his mind for what was to be expected of him.

Sonder began to contemplate if this plan of theirs would work...or. He didn't want to think about that possibility at the moment. Behind the crew (which were all wearing black parka-like jackets with a crudely-applied spray paint decal of a vector wolf's head on their backs), Maelo was suited up in a type of armor for dogs (with emergency ration snacks in pouches around his waist) and had a parachute attached to his back.

"When I give the word, we jump!" yelled Captain Raizar. "Yes, sir!" Orfa, Klay, and Sonder yelled back in replying unison. "That's what I like to hear." Raizar said to himself. "JUMP!" the *Vector Wolves'* captain bellowed at the top of his lungs, ushering them all down the ramp and off of the *Nameless Maiden*, which was currently hovering over a plateau-world whose surface was entirely made-up of jagged blood-red mountains and immensely deep valleys, made only all the more horrifying by the gloomy light the ship's amber-tinted flares were giving off.

A blast of rock 'n' roll music was sent out after them, indicating that Mason had gone to her happy place in this moment as a way to keep her cool. Beyond the ship's flares radius was complete and utter darkness, and an enormous energy crystal that was covered up by a strange, stringy, black sinew that siphoned and smothered its light and heat loomed above them in the sky. As the *Vector Wolves* dropped down, the ice-cold temperature of the world set in, causing a subtle frost to set in on their bodies.

Then, at the last moment, as the ground came rushing up at them, they activated their booster-packs, which fired out two blasts of concentrated, propellant energy, saving them from being smashed-apart by the gravity of the realm. The *Nameless Maiden* took to higher skies after this, and Mason pulled the vehicle into a barrel-roll before careening around in a 'U'-bend and rocketing past them. On their wrist-worn comms devices, Mason spoke to them. "Sound off! Call your signs so I know you made it!" she yelled. "*Red!*" "*BLUE.*" "*Stripes!*" "*Snow!*" "And *me!*" Captain Raizar yelled in reply after the others had finished, then smirked as he turned to look at them. The tiny lamps on the sides of his head were blinding to look at. Then, Klay and Sonder caught Maelo, who had parachuted down and placed him and his boot-covered paws on the ground.

"Right, let's make this clean and fast. It's a hit-and-run operation. Stick close to me and be ready to fight for your lives. Remember, the fate of the world is ours to decide." he then turned and said to them. "*Stripes*, start us off, please." "Yes, sir!" Orfa said in response, and then drew out the knell. "*Snow*, you next!" Raizar ordered Sonder. "Uh, yes, sir." he said, not being used to the militaristic drills Raizar was issuing out. The man was *razor*-sharp when sobered. The white-haired worker walked over to Orfa and allowed his hand to be nicked for the sake of the weapon activating. As he bled onto the dagger, its runes began to glow, and the knell (as if by magic) became a sword and Sonder pulled at it, dispensing energy copies of the weapon of varying type and size, which he provided the others. Maelo was even gifted a double-sided one to wield with his mouth.

Then, they ditched the parachute after disconnecting it and stepped back from the vector wolf, and in a flash, the animal grew far larger in size and started glowing, and the seams of the armor stretched to meet this demand. "Alright then, now we're cooking with oil!" Raizar said in response as he witnessed this happen. Then, he snapped his fingers, and Maelo snapped to attention before budding off into twelve other separate forms; the most amount he could maintain at a time for prolonged periods, such as the highly experimental and exceedingly dangerous excursion they were currently on. For all they knew, they could all die here. But, they decided that this was not the outcome they would allow to come to fruition if they could help it.

The Vector Wolves mounted their vector wolves and then began to charge forward as Captain Raizar gave the word. "Charge!" he bellowed, and Orfa joined in by letting out a howl. The glowing sea of giant canines was like a river pouring down the side of the floating plateau, and in a near-instant they were gunning it past countless thousands of Unwilling, reducing them to bluish powder with the weapons.

The invasive force of freedom fighters launched immediately into action, mowing down each and every Unwilling they came across with the outstretched blades of energy, occasionally uttering: "rest in peace." to pay respects to the dead that were consumed by Ahz-Mund and soothe their consciences. "Was it really smart to come down here without any guaranteed back up?!" Sonder asked Raizar. "They'll come, my friends, I promise!" Raizar yelled in his usual colorfully-toned accent. "Besides; we're wanted men now!" he explained and then chuckled. This drew an expression of shock out of Klay and Sonder. Orfa's face remained stagnant; she was solely focused on staying alive and keeping the others alive while she's at it.

The ferocity had yet to fully come out to play. In her hands were two smaller versions of the knell made of pure energy that she held backwards. It seemed to be her preferred choice of how she wielded them as she methodically carved apart the Unwilling that crossed her path. Within the first minutes of this assault, they had cleared out an exceptionally large number of the undead, thoroughly impressing the Vector Wolves with the idea that victory might actually be a possibility against such forces.

Right as they thought that, a surge of stronger, larger undead appeared from out of the ground. They had large great-swords, halberds, and war hammers in their grasp, and they gave the Vector Wolves a run for their money. "You guys doin' okay?!" Jasper asked over the comms devices with the wavering uncertainty of a motherly person. "We will be, just need to take out the bigger ones now. Shouldn't be a problem!" explained Raizar as he and the others continued to mow down the legions of undead soldiers that were under the necromancer's influence.

Then, an even bigger problem arose in the skies above. "Uh, guys?! We're fenced in!" Mason yelled over comms, indicating the arrival of dozens of ribcage ships that began to hover around the plateau's top. "Oh...*Fates.*" Raizar said to himself quietly as he looked upon the sight. He then mustered his courage and turned back to face the others. "We're going to do this! Do you hear me?!" he cried to them as the world went whistling by them all. "Sir, yes, sir!" they yelled back at him, looking mightily terrified by this reality. "We keep going, and keep your focus on what's ahead of you!" Captain Raizar then yelled as he returned his eyes to the front, where countless more Unwilling were being put to rest by theirs and Maelo's blades. Bluish ash sprayed by like dust in a dust storm, covering their skin with the substance.

"Ack! We shoulda worn masks!" Klay yelled in disgust and frustration. The others weren't exactly having fun with this either. "This should be plenty enough to grab their attention." said Raizar. Then, the tides turned, and the

Unwilling that had been chasing them had suddenly caught up, pressing the Vector Wolves up the side of a mountain, only for them to arrive at the lip of a cliff with a terrifying drop. "Heel, heel!" Raizar yelled, causing all of Maelo's clones to grind to a halt just before they would have run right off the edge of the cliff. Sonder, Klay, and Orfa's eyes had widened during this, and all they could do was look back at the approaching waves of undead with horror as they sat atop the energy beasts.

"Dive!" Raizar ordered, and he led them all down the side of the cliff, the feet of the Vector Wolves seemingly magnetizing to the rock wall and keeping everyone from falling off. "Now!" Captain Raizar barked, and the wolves launched off of the side, easily evading the waterfall of Unwilling that fell behind them. Then, when they had reached the bottom of the canyon, they continued running until reaching a point to climb back up and out of. "Snow, take 'em out!" commanded Raizar, and Sonder followed this by creating a bow from out of the knell he held and, using another knell (shaped like a sword), combined it with the other and began to fire off explosive energy shots down into the recesses of the canyon's valley below them, wiping out the undead.

"Excellent work, my friends! Excellent work. Let's keep going!" hollered Captain Raizar, and for a brief moment, the Vector Wolves with him all smiled. Then, suddenly, a single ship appeared in the sky above. *It was not the Nameless Maiden*. This surprised them all, but the Vector Wolves soon took on a look of excitement as they witnessed its arrival. "Look! They're here!" cried Sonder. "Just as Ozo said they might." remarked Klay, who was grinning for the first time (to

Sonder's knowledge). The avian-styled ship (which bore a smoother, more modernly-painted body) had an emblem on the side of it that was much like the white vector wolf insignia that now adorned the *Nameless Maiden*'s sides, only, it was of a lizard wielding an axe in its mouth.

"It's Team 7!" Raizar yelled triumphantly, as though he was presenting them. The glee and relief on the captain's face was enough to make Sonder chuckle with gladness. But, he knew that it would be short-lived, as they still had an entire rest of a plateau and its kiln of radiance to liberate. Then, things got serious when they attempted to drop off their troops. The Vector Wolves screeched to a halt when they watched a group of Unwilling launch themselves at the ship, which flew off into the air with them still attached to its hull just as they delivered their shore team safely to the ground. On their wrist-worn comms devices, the members of Team 7 were arguing back and forth. Then, the men whose identities were being obscured by darkness, approached the Vector Wolves.

"Captain Raizar of Team 9?!" the lead silhouetted man called out. "Yes?" Raizar answered. "Let's have it. The weapon. Give it to me." said the voice. "I can't let you just take it from us, *Sloane*." Raizar fired back like a rebellious cowboy that was giving the town sheriff a hard time. "And why not? It's only fair, after all. You did snake a score out from under us a few days ago." replied Sloane. Klay made a guilty face when he heard this.

Under the light of the flares and the glow from the vector wolves, Sonder could see that Sloane was a man who had dark skin, spiky silver hair, and what looked like a metal plate covering his eyes. He wore black battle armor with a silver shoulder pad. In his hands was an automatic repeating rifle. A cape on his back flapped in the wind behind him The bottom of Raizar's trench coat did the same. "Well, first come, first serve. That's what I always say." Raizar said irresponsibly with a grin. It looked as though the two men were about to have a stand-off.

Sonder became immensely troubled by this, as Captain Raizar had previously assured everyone that their ties with Team 7 would be receptive and helpful. It dawned on him that this might have been the captain exaggerating or taking his alliances for granted. Either way, the tension between the two men was severe, and everyone started to sweat as Sloane prepared to raise the gun and Raizar drew out his revolver and braced himself.

"Nah, I'm jus' kidding. We're here to help." Sloane said as he suddenly assumed a more easygoing and whimsical demeanor. "Good. That's a relief. Well, we have plenty to go around. Snow, would you be kind enough to arm this man and his men?" the Captain then asked the white-haired worker.

Then, he looked down at the head of the vector wolf he was riding atop and asked: "Maelo, you remember Sloane, yes?" Raizar asked the main dog, who was indicated by a fluffy mane that had grown on his back thanks to the Knell's powers. Every one of the large dogs' tails wagged in excitement at this. Then, three of them walked over to Sloane and allowed him and his companions to climb up and ride them.

"Ingram, get *The Duchess* out of here and to safety. We've met up with Raizar and his crew." Sloane then said into his wrist. "Copy that!" the voice on his wrist called back to him. "I'm Sloane Sinclaire, this here is Fern and this is Erd." the unpredictable man said and gestured to the other two in his company—one was a ginger-haired girl and the other looked like a somewhat nerdy fellow that had brown hair, rounded glasses, and a fluffy beard.

"Well met, this is Sonder, Klay, and Orfa." the captain pointed to each in the wrong order. "Ah, well met, you guys. This is so exciting!" Sloane said with a giddy expression on his face. "Just remember though, 'Ozo', what happens if you fail here today." Sloane cautioned as he became more serious. "My friend, we won't be failing today." Raizar said confidently to Sloane, who then took on a serious expression. Sonder began to wonder how the man could see with the metal plate over his eyes.

"Let's win the day, then." said Sloane as he held out his hand towards Raizar, who met this with his own hand and the two had a squeeze-shake before he and Sloane parted ways, turning on their heels and beginning to move in the opposite direction. "We'll attack from both sides, yeah?" Slone asked Raizar. "Sounds good to me, partner." Raizar said back. "Do they have a cool call-sign like ours?" Sonder asked the captain. Behind him, Sloane had heard this and spoke up when he issued out a reply.

"We're the *Steel Qobolds*." Sloane said proudly and with a wide smile as he gestured to the silver plating of their shoulder pads, as if this, like the wolf artwork on the Vector Wolves' jackets, was their signifier. "We were going about traveling the *Maelstrom* and its realms and we've been trying to hunt down Saurossian patrols, hence the name." Sloane explained. "Wait, really? The three of you manage that all by yourselves?" Klay asked. "It's not always about the numbers, kid. It's about what you do with what you've got;

that's what really counts and matters." replied
Sloane. "Captain Raizar here tells me you guys
had a run in with one of their dreadnoughts?" he
then asked. "Yeah, we did." explained Klay.
"Wait, you four go out and fight Saurossians?
There were seven of us when we got
overwhelmed, how do you guys manage not to?"
Sonder asked Sloane. "It's easy; just gotta know
how to hunt 'em." he explained.

"We do not have time for small talk!"
yelled Orfa, who then led the other Vector Wolves
and the Steel Qobolds to the edge of the plateau,
circling around, and in another few long moments
cleared out the entirety of the plateau's surface of
Unwilling. This was then re-populated by the bone
ships above. "Damn it!" yelled Klay, sounding
mightily upset in the moment. "We've got this,
just keep going, my friends!" urged Raizar who,
like the others, was already starting to become

exhausted by this effort. "We need more men!" yelled Sloane.

"It's fine, just keep your head down and stay on your toes. We can do this! We have to stall for time!" Raizar reassured them. "That's even *if* they heard us..." Klay said to himself. It was loud enough for Sonder to hear. The glowing young man looked over and shot him a look with his lamp-like eyes. "What?" Klay asked. "Let's move, we've nearly got them!" cried Captain Raizar as they continued to clear out the surface of Unwilling.

This was then rudely interrupted by the arrival of Mund-Karr-Mudgeon, who crashed down upon them, causing one of the Steel Qobolds to fall off of a Maelo clone and roll over to the grounded shadow drake, which loosed an ear-splittingly loud roar that rocked the earth beneath their feet. The beast then looked down at its prey with hungry eyes. The Steel Qobold lifted her arms out to try and protect herself, but the effort was wasted. The dragon stepped forward and snapped its head down, retrieving Fern in its mouth. The poor, frightened girl then disappeared down its glowing gullet, which snapped shut as the dragon swallowed her and then turned to look at the survivors slowly as it loosed a long, guttural belch. They were all horrified by what they had just seen.

"Fern! No!" cried Sloane, who began to steer his Maelo clone back around towards the beast. "Slone, no! Get back!" Raizar urged him, fearing for his friend's life. "Give her back, you big bastard!" cried Sloane as he launched off of the giant energy wolf and aimed the copy of the Knell he held in his hands down towards the dragon's throat. Sloane split it wide open, causing the beast to shriek out in pain.

Then, Sloane reached into its opened throat and pulled Fern back out by the arm as the dragon withdrew from the two of them. He had managed to save her before she could be turned undead or worse—*digested*. They were all impressed with the man's quick save. Mund-Karr-Mudgeon retreated as its wounds healed back up. "What gives? Shouldn't it be powder by now?" Klay asked. "I didn't think to chance it earlier." said Sonder, referring to when they had first encountered the winged monster. Sloane placed the slimed-up girl in front of him on the copy of Maelo and yelled out to get the dog moving.

As they picked up speed once again, they could hear the draconic beast crying out in the distance behind them. "Keep going! We'll head down onto the lower hemisphere now!" ordered Raizar. Maelo and his clones doubled their efforts to carry the Vector Wolves and Steel Qobolds to the safety of the upside-down mountainous region that lay beneath a floating plateau's main surface. Once there, they realized the mistake they had just made. "Guys, no! Stick to the top region!" Mason urged them over the comms device channel.

"Why? Why's that?! Repeat, over!" said Klay. "Because, uh well…" Mason started to say as she witnessed countless thousands of undead pour out from craters in the plateau's bottom's surface. "Uh-oh…" Klay said out loud as fear began to take him. "No! Keep calm and be confident in this plan. We can still do this!" Raizar urged the rusty-red-haired man. "We need to cover more ground to if we're to snuff these things out fast enough!" "Right!" Klay said in response. "It's all going to be okay, and if it isn't, we'll keep fighting until it is okay! Stay alive, all of you! Spread out and take 'em down!" Captain Raizar bellowed before giving the copy of Maelo he was riding upon a firm bump with his foot, which sent the creature into a charge towards the amassing armies of strong undead.

The others behind him followed suit and picked up speed to line up next to him on both sides with their weapons raised and poised for more battle. Then, just before the wave of Unwilling crashed against them, they fanned out and broke off into groups, avoiding being overtaken by them and causing the horde to stumble over itself as the rushing undead foot soldiers struggled with their stopping power. Sonder was with Klay, Ayb with Orfa, and Raizar was with Sloane and his two Qobolds. When they happened upon the raised up sides of the caldera they were in, the Vector Wolves they were riding began to move up the sides and towards the top.

Once there, they could see what looked like an enormous, castle-like structure off in the distance, which was illuminated by stray bolts of lightning that Mund-Karr-Mudgeon was giving off. The black-winged beast soared past the castle tower and bellowed into the night sky, a terrible sound that made the resistance fighters lower their heads and cup their hands over their ears.

"Someone's gotta take that thing out!" cried Klay. "I know, but how?!" asked Sonder, who wracked his brain for a moment. Then, the memory of him using the weapon to fire out a blast of energy on top of the *Nameless Maiden* came flooding back. Looking down at the energized weapon, Sonder contemplated how he would go about doing something like that again, or if it would even work this time with them already using a great deal of its power for the copies of Maelo and the swords. A sudden determination came over him, and he turned to face Klay once more. "Get me to Orfa!" he yelled. The rusty-red-haired man nodded and made the vector wolf he was riding peel away off to the side. Sonder's followed closely after. They had to fight their way through a sea of glowing-eyed undead to get to her.

Luckily, Ayb was with her, allowing for Klay and Sonder to easily keep track of where they were, thanks to the reflective blue plating on its chassis. "Orfa!" Sonder called to the striped girl, who was laser-focused on the kills she was making with her twin blades of energy. This snapped her out of the moment, and she looked over in the direction that she had heard Sonder's voice. "Over here! We gotta take out the dragon!" Sonder urged her. With a nod of acknowledgment, the Yarggen Clan girl pulled her copy of Maelo away and towards the two of them. Ayb followed behind her on a wolf of his own. Just then, an immensely large undead came out from a crater in the ground and jumped at Sonder and Klay, causing them to fall off of their magic mounts. They hit the ground hard, and the undead gave them no pause as it bore down on them like a berserker with its halberd.

Brushing off the sting of his new bruises, Klay quickly leapt up and out of the way of the flurried attacks, and Sonder rolled away to safety. However, he realized all too late that he had dropped the knell when he fell off of Maelo, and he could see that the weapon was now under the shadow of the halberd-wielding undead, who loomed above him with its weapon raised and a glint of malice in its glowing eyes. In the nick of time, Ayb rushed in with his boosters, slamming right into the giant and repeatedly stabbing it with his copy of the knell until it exploded into ash-powder, saving Sonder and Klay. "Phew! Thanks for the save!" Sonder said to Ayb. "That's three." said the mechanical being. Sonder shook his head and smiled at this.

Klay jogged over, reached down and pulled Sonder onto his feet. It was then that Orfa had arrived. "Are you alright?!" asked the striped girl, who sounded concerned. "Yeah, we're fine, thanks to Ayb here." said Sonder, who retrieved the knell from off the ground. "Good. What did you need?" Orfa then asked. Sonder turned and pointed up to the stormy skies, where they could see the shadow of the dragon as it flew through the dark clouds.

"We gotta do something about that." Sonder explained to her. "Agreed." said Orfa, who then nodded and steeled herself atop the wolf. Sonder and Klay got back onto theirs and the four of them started to move towards the dragon with a springy step. "What's the plan?!" Orfa asked, having to yell over the rushing wind as it blew past them. "Just get me close enough. I think I can channel the energy into our weapons and we can blast it together!" Sonder explained, having to yell as well. "Understood." Orfa said as she gave a nod before returning her attention to what was in front of them.

Another wave of undead surged towards the quartet of Vector Wolves, who used their energy weapons to make short work of them. "Ayb, how are you holding up?" Klay asked the synthform. "My hull's integrity has held up in worse conditions; I am fine." the robotic being answered. "Good." Klay said in response.

As they neared the dragon, which was slowing down and lowering itself back into the battlefield, it reared back as it hovered and blasted the nearby area with a concentrated beam of violet flame. "Whoa!" Sonder reacted instinctively and pulled back on Maelo to slow down. The others did the same behind him. Mund-Karr-Mudgeon was firing down at Sloane and Raizar, who were ahead. The two were doing well to evade this attack, but the unfortunate Qobold that lagged behind them, Erd, was reduced to a charred skeleton after the breath passed over him for but a split second. The copy of Maelo disappeared into nothingness as well. The dragon also managed to char some of the undead around him.

Then, those same Unwilling got back up and went over to the Qobold's skeletal remains, where they then vomited their shadows onto him. A moment later, the skeletal Erd stood once more, only this time with that same eerie glow in his eyes as the other undead.

"No! Erd!" Sloane cried, lamenting the fate of his dear friend and teammate. "Damn!" Klay cursed under his breath. "Orfa, stay close to me, you guys spread out and try to draw its fire!" Sonder ordered, taking the initiative. "Right." said Orfa. Klay and Ayb nodded before following the orders.

Drawing closer to the dragon, they watched as it zeroed in on Raizar and Sloane, who had brought on its full aggro. The beast flapped its wings about wildly as it sent out short, burst-like blasts of purple fire at them. The pair dodged out of the way just in time with each one. Deeming that they were indeed close enough, Sonder reached out to Orfa with one hand and raised up the knell with his other.

"Orfa! Now!" he barked, and the striped girl reached over to him and took her hand in his. Her skin was surprisingly cold to the touch, as if her blood ran colder than the others. Then, the glow that his body was giving off was transferred partly to her, and the runes on their weapons began to glow blindingly bright as Sonder concentrated his powers into them. "We'll probably only get one shot at this; don't miss!" Sonder yelled. "Right!" she yelled back. Just as

Mund-Karr-Mudgeon was bearing down on Sloane and Fern, who were still sharing a vector wolf mount, Sonder and Orfa channeled their weapons' energy and fired off a massive burst towards the dragon.

It was as if they had made a railgun using the knells. The exceedingly bright blast of energy sheared right past the dragon, who dodged out of the way at the last second. However, they had managed to damage one of its wings, which now was torn up with several holes from the blast. This caused the beast to shriek out in pain before it flew away and then crashed to the ground some distance away. "Yeah! We got it!" Sonder yelled triumphantly. Orfa looked impressed by this, and she found herself smiling. *Maybe they really could pull this off.* She thought to herself.

It was then that the dragon drew itself back up into the sky and then came smashing down onto Raizar and Sloane, casting them aside in other directions as their copies of Maelo and Fern were crushed under the weight of the otherworldly beast. Fern's screams were silenced as she was reduced to a bloody paste.

"Oh shit!" Klay cursed. The shockwave of this sent the others flying off of their mounts and rolling off of the sides of cliffs and then into ditches of coarse dirt. "Ah, damn it!" Klay continued cursing. Then, he turned to see a skeletal monstrosity in the shape of a rat that was poised to bite him with its giant incisors.

Managing to avoid this by throwing himself to the side and then guarding the attacks with the copy of the knell in his hands. He quickly drew out a shield from the weapon, guarded against a second attack, then withdrew, stood, and took to a battle stance that even managed to startle the rat, which recoiled at the side of the weaponry.

"Yeah, you know what these are, don't ya?" Klay asked the mass of combined bones with a skull for a face in a mocking tone as his lip pulled into a grin.

Then, behind the one, dozens of others began to emerge in the darkness. "Oh no..." Klay muttered. At the sight of this, his demeanor fell to one that revealed just how exhausted he was. Then, Orfa arrived behind him to back him up with the daggers she had shifted to being bladed knuckle dusters with some manipulation of the radiance. She truly appeared to be like a wild beast as she bared her fangs, got on all-fours, and growled loudly at the horde of rats like a territorial animal.

Instinctively, Klay stepped over to her and then hid behind her. She shot him a look of slight disbelief with her golden, cat-like eyes, which he returned with a guilty look. Standing together, they then fought through the legion of rats with the help of the Maelo clones, who had just recovered from the shockwave and rushed overhead to meet the undead amalgamations head on.

Far-off, Sonder stood and groaned from how much pain he was now in, and after looking himself over realized just how dinged-up he had been since the start of this whole thing. He wondered when he would catch a break as his ears buzzed with ringing. His head was splitting, and everything hurt. To his right, he could see that Ayb had been knocked out once again, bearing a similar dent in his camera-like head. "Aw, come on, Ayb." Sonder muttered to himself as he shook his head. Ahead of him, he witnessed Sloane being assaulted by enemies similar to what Klay and Orfa were dealing with. "Uh-oh..." Sonder then said aloud as he turned on his heel just in time to meet the fangs of one of the deadly, rat-like shapes that the necromancer had assembled. Bringing the knell up relatively in time, Sonder managed to save himself from the brunt of the attack.

However, he knocked flat onto his back and then was nicked by the talons of a skeletal rat on his ankles, which were the only unprotected part of his body under the large, blocky shield of energy. Thinking to experiment, Sonder turned his sword into a chainsword. The chain of which actually worked. Though, this shape was harder for Sonder to maintain, as it made him feel slightly anemic from how much energy it had to draw out from him in order to work.

Swinging it left-and-right, Sonder quickly eliminated the skeletal rodents with the weapon he had conjured. Then, he found his footing once again and braced himself for further attack. Up above, in the sky, Jasper and Mason had a problem of their own, as a small handful of Unwilling had dropped down from the ribcages and onto the top of the ship. "Damn it, not again. Get the hell off my ship!" Mason yelled. "What do we do? We don't have any weapons!" Jasper exclaimed. He was becoming frantic as the Unwilling atop the ship began to pry and tear their way inside.

"Hold on to something!" Mason yelled back to Jasper, who then grabbed ahold of the back of a chair as the pilot swung the ship side-to-side, shaking off some of the zombies. "That's doing the trick!" said Jasper. "We're not clear yet, strap in!" Mason ordered him, and the freckled boy climbed into a chair and buckled himself to it right in time for Mason to pull off a series of rolls through the air. This shook loose the rest of the Unwilling from the ship's outer hull. The pair breathed a sigh of relief. Then, they were both startled by the door to the bridge sliding open. Turning to see who it was, they were horrified to see a rotting corpse with glowing eyes staring them down as it held itself upright by holding onto the doorway with its lifeless hands.

"Oh shit!" Mason cursed. Jasper went as white as a ghost. It then began to shamble over to them, prompting Jasper to jump out of his chair and retrieve the nearest object he could use to protect himself with—a maintenance pipe that had been switched out when Mason and Klay had repaired the engines. The pilot drew out her handgun and fired off a few rounds in an attempt to halt its advance. Though it was bleeding, the undead looked to be unaffected by the bullets.

It then launched into a hobbled run or sorts straight at Jasper, who instinctively swung the pipe in self defense. It knocked the undead to the side, where it fell onto the controls of the pilot's stereo system. The rock 'n' roll music was made louder by it falling against the volume knob, something that made the undead freeze up. It looked like the loud music was having some kind of effect on it. Thinking to chance it, Jasper hooked the undead around the neck with the elbow of the pipe and pulled it into a run back out through the bridge door.

He then yelled at the top of his lungs as he did this, and he pumped his legs as hard as he could make them move. Without stopping, Jasper then pulled the protesting zombie all the way into the ramp room, where he threw it down onto the ground with a swing of the pipe. Then, he rushed over to the ramp controls and keyed in the button to lower the ramp. Once it was opened wide enough, Jasper then kicked the undead a few times until it was sent flying out the ship's back. Jasper then closed the ramp back up and returned to the hall, where he found that the roof hatch had been opened, and he closed this as well. He then moved back into the cockpit bridge, where a thoroughly impressed Mason awaited him.

"Well, damn. I didn't know you had it in you, Jasper." she commented. "Did you notice how it seemed to be affected by the music?" Jasper asked Mason. "Yeah, I did." Mason answered. She then switched on her comms device and spoke into it. "This is Mason, listen, the Unwilling are affected by loud music. It seems to slow them down!" "That's good, but what use is that now?" Sloane asked Raizar, overhearing the girl over the captain's comms device.

Then, Sonder's eyes widened as he remembered the cassette player in his pocket. Retrieving it, he then used his abilities to power it on and make it as loud as possible, causing it to shriek with feedback as the best part of the song he had tried listening to back when began to ring out.

The large, rat-like clumps of bone and sinew paused at the sound of it, allowing for them to be taken out with ease by Klay and the others. It was then that Sonder took note of Captain Raizar, who was standing close to the downed dragon. Then, the beast's ribs opened up, and Dey-Ud-Mund crawled out.

The dragon's wings surrounded him as he stepped out from the monster's chest, clothing him with a protective robe of darkness. Clad in his usual helmet and armed with a knell of his own, the flame-eyed villain posed before the captain with an imposing and intimidating stance. Captain Raizar froze and locked his eyes onto the helmeted figure with a burning hatred. The time had come; *he would finally have his chance at revenge.* As he began to walk towards Dey-Ud-Mund, his footsteps became heavier, and his pace quickened until he broke into a full-blown sprint towards the dark specter as a primal yell loosed from deep within him. Bringing the copy of the knell upwards, Raizar then slammed it down onto Dey-Ud-Mund, who blocked the attack with a firm guard of his raised sword. The weapons rang out like the thundering blast of a cannon as they met. The duel that Raizar had always dreamed of had begun at last.

"You took them from me." Raizar said to the helmeted, flaming-eyed man. "My home." Raizar smashed the knell onto the shade's guard a second time. "My wife." he said with growing anger and sorrow as he slammed the weapon down hard like a hammer. Dey-Ud-Mund was on the defensive, moving back little by little as Raizar pressed his attack. "My son!" yelled Raizar as he brought it down again even harder. Tears began to stream down his face. "Everything I ever loved is gone because of you!" *SLAM!* "I will destroy you!" *SLAM!* "I will put an end to your hellish dominion!" *SLAM!* Raizar drew up to his full height, pausing for just a moment. "And when you're gone, I will dance like a madman on your graves." he spat with venom before launching back into his attack. Sonder was stunned as he witnessed the duel.

Unsure of how to help (as he didn't want to get in the captain's way), he simply stood in place, taken by the spectacle. "Sonder! Where's Raizar?!" Klay cried out to him via the comm-link. Sonder lifted it up and spoke into it. "He found him. *Dey-Ud-Mund*. He's taking him on alone." he explained. The silence on the other end of the line confirmed that Klay, too, was unsure of how to proceed. "Stay where you are, we'll come to you!" Klay then yelled. Sonder's positional data on their wrist-worn devices would lead them to his location. As the duel progressed, the captain of the

Vector Wolves forced Dey-Ud-Mund into a retreat across craggy hills, a stony bridge, and then inside the crumbling, flare-lit crimson castle tower at the bottom of the plateau, whose gravity made only some sense to the resistance fighters. It behaved much in the same way as planets, and yet it was all so strange and magical. It was as if it had been dreamt up for a children's fantasy tale.

When Raizar disappeared through the entrance in pursuit, Sonder decided to follow after them, entering into the giant, crimson structure with a firm grip on the knell. The place was ancient and reeked of old death. Following the sounds of meeting metal, Sonder quickened his pace as he ran through the interior of the gloomy castle. What Sonder witnessed next was the most striking and heavy-handed sword duel in his lifetime. The captain was fighting with every last ounce of rage that he carried in his body. With the alcohol in his system from the previous night acting also as a manner of fuel for his hatred, Raizar bore down onto the helmeted shade's defenses with reckless abandon. But, there was form and power to each swing, stab, and riposte. The combatants managed to stare unblinkingly into each other's eyes as the duel progressed.

Raizar pressed Dey-Ud-Mund on the retreat multiple times; up stairs, through halls of confined spaces that neither fighter could do much with, and also across the floors of a broken-up ballroom from ages long passed. Sonder tailed them until they reached the roof of the castle, which had three towers at its end. He considered making a bow and arrow out of the knell, but feared that he might miss and hit Raizar instead of the helmeted shade.

The middle tower was taller than the other two, and in front of it was a strange shape that resembled an altar. It had a slot for a sword blade in its center. This was set above a large orange gem with an eerie light inside it that pulsed gently. Sonder had no clue what it was. Captain Raizar was still engaged in close combat with Dey-Ud-Mund, who appeared to be getting tired from how persistent of a battler the man was. He hadn't once given the shade a chance of retaliating.

This was a completely one-sided fight. It even looked like the captain was prolonging the duel intentionally in order to savor the kill. He truly resembled a wolf playing with its food in that moment. Sonder felt as though this wasn't going to last long, and that Raizar was only tiring himself out in the process. It was as if he was burning every last fiber of the pain he had been burdened with after the tragedy that had struck his life many years ago into his swings, stabs, and smashes. He wasn't letting up anytime soon, either, evidenced by him boxing in Dey-Ud-Mund near the crystal and the slotted altar.

Then, Captain Raizar pulled back and yelled as he began to plunge his copy of the knell towards the helmeted shade. Just as it was about to connect, the captain was run-through by Dey-Ud-Mund. Sonder dove right into action, screaming: "Noooo!" all the way over to them as he ran. Captain Raizar fell away to the ground and dropped the knell copy, causing it to shatter apart and then evaporate into nothingness.

Then, Sonder put up a decent fight against the helmeted shade for a short time. He even managed to get a good lick in with the knell, cutting Dey-Ud-Mund across the stomach. But, instead of falling away to ash, the distracted shade's cut healed instantly, shocking Sonder. His lack of fighting experience and understanding led to his footing slipping, and the helmeted shade pressed his advantage and took the opportunity, hitting the white-haired worker hard in the gut with the bottom of his weapon.

This caused him to fall to his knees before keeling over. Wincing through the pain, Sonder looked up at the burning-eyed man with a look of hatred. Dey-Ud-Mund then lifted up his weapon and poised it for impaling Sonder. Just before he could do so, Orfa came up from out of nowhere and swung her knell copy, which she had morphed into a hammer at Dey-Ud-Mund's head, throwing the shade hard to the ground and sending his crumpled helmet flying to the side.

A bright flash went off as his body made impact with the ground, stunning everyone for a brief moment. Once her eyes adjusted, Orfa moved in to finish him off and make the kill with the bottom of the weapon (reconfigured to a sword) in a stabbing fashion, but was stopped by

Sonder. "Wait!" he cried to her. "I need to know something first." he explained as he got up and walked over to Dey-Ud-Mund. When Orfa and Sonder looked to see his identity, they were completely shocked to see that *it was Sonder*. Or, at least, a man that looked strikingly like him—with stark-white hair and all.

Sonder felt a deeply uncomfortable pit form in his stomach. "What?" Sonder asked aloud. His mind felt ready to break. The question of whether there was a possibility of there being multiple of the same person in the multiverse bubbled up in Sonder's head, something he would be sure to ask the others about it later. Orfa was troubled by this revelation as well. But, before they could do anything, Mund-Karr-Mudgeon had appeared at the top of the castle's tower and, in a flash, it took Dey-Ud-Mund's body into its talons, roared at the pair, and flew up into the atmosphere and disappeared into the black mist beyond, leaving the helmet and the sword with the orange gem set into its guard behind. Orfa and Sonder became frantic, not knowing what to do about this. It had all happened incredibly fast. All she could do was show him a face of deep confusion, something he returned in a nearly-identical fashion.

There was also a newfound sense of distrust between the two of them. Orfa decided she would bury this for the time being, but a great many questions about her host had cropped up in her mind after making this strange discovery. Then, Mason's voice called out to them on their wrist-worn comms devices, breaking the tension. "Guys? What's going on?!" asked the golden-haired pilot. Orfa and Sonder exchanged a look. "Captain Raizar is down; he's been injured. Dey-Ud-Mund and his *pet* got away." Sonder explained to her as he and Orfa looked over Captain Raizar, who wasn't looking very good. Silence filled the line for a moment. "Damn it..." Mason then said, sounding mournful. Captain Raizar pointed weakly over to the altar and then seized Sonder's sword hand, communicating what needed to be done.

"Sonder!" Orfa said as she joined in on pointing over at the altar. She was cradling Raizar in her arms. "Right." Sonder said in reply, then moved over to the object and picked up Dey-Ud-Mund's knell. He could see that there was a slot wide enough for a sword's blade, and instinctively, he plugged the weapon into it. An incredibly powerful burst of energy surged through him as he held onto the weapon. Its crystal and runes started to take on a blindingly bright, white glow. Something in his mind told him to turn the weapon, as if it were something he'd done before, and in doing so, he caused a blast of radiance to fire up and directly towards the covered-up Kiln that clung to the sky like a bolt of lightning, melting away the blackened sinew that smothered its light and cracking the orange crystal that was underneath the altar. The bolt then branched off and completely wiped out every single one of the ribcage ships above.

Strangely enough, none of this hurt him, something he hadn't expected. As a matter-of-fact, Sonder felt strong and empowered by the energy. To him, it was like a wellspring that healed and renewed him. With the last of the sinew melted away, the bone ships destroyed, and the Unwilling completely laid to rest, Sonder turned the knell back to its entry position and withdrew it from the altar. The light of the Kiln began to flood the world with heat and colorful vibrancy. Sonder and Orfa stared up at it in amazement.

"Wow..." Sonder said under his breath as he looked upon the sight. "Whatever you guys just did, it looks like it's working." Klay said over the comms. Then, Raizar made a sound that prompted Sonder and Orfa's attention to return to him. "We need to move him. He needs medical attention." the striped girl said quickly, taking the initiative. "Right." Sonder said in reply before moving over and helping her carry Raizar. "Mason! We need a pickup!" Sonder called to her on the comms device. "Stay where you are, I'm pinpointing your location!" she answered.

After a few short moments, the *Nameless Maiden* careened through the air and then slowed when it had reached the tower's top. The ship then hovered near one of the towers' balconies using a set of boosters on its underside, its ramp opened and lowered just enough to receive them. Being as careful as they could be, Orfa and Sonder dragged

Captain Raizar's body up and out into the balcony. When they had reached it, Raizar threw himself about and groaned, drawing the attention of the pair that were carrying him. When they looked down at him, he simply said: "Put me down here." He had managed to get this out through ragged breaths.

Obeying their commanding officer's orders, Orfa and Sonder propped up the captain against the wall of the balcony, where he had a great view of the kiln's burgeoning, amber-colored light. Though they were at the very peak of the bottom of the plateau, they could still see the crystal high up and far off. It seemed to have a cycle of sorts similar to that of a sun; rising during daytime, falling away to its bottom by night time. "What's going on?!" Jasper asked, calling out to them from inside the ramp room of the *Nameless Maiden*. "The Captain's dying." The words escaped

Sonder's mouth before he even had time to process them. Jasper's emerald-colored eyes widened with sadness when he heard this.

"Get Mason." Sonder ordered Jasper, who remained fixed in place from being overwhelmed with emotion. "Jasper, get Mason!" Sonder yelled, snapping him back to reality. The thin and short boy turned and scampered back inside the ship at this, and Sonder turned his attention back to the dying captain. By now, Klay, Sloane, and a repaired Ayb had managed to join them at the tower's top. As soon as they saw what was up, it shocked them.

For all the time they'd known Captain Raizar, they didn't think that this would be where he would meet his fate. With the ship on autopilot, Mason and Jasper rushed out and onto the balcony and froze as they looked upon their fallen friend. Pain stung their heart strings as the man they'd respected and revered was slowly leaving their world.

"Man, this sucks..." Captain Raizar started to say. "I was really hoping I'd get to see all of you grow..." he continued as he looked up at each of the crewmates. "Like little trees..." the man then turned slowly over to Sonder. "Take care of them, *Snow*. Don't get...too caught up in...getting square with this world..." said Raizar as his eyes began to dull over.

Sonder had gone numb due to how overwhelmed he felt, and as such, found that he was speechless. Jasper took on a look of anguish and sorrow as his tears fell. Klay turned away and bit hard down on his lip as he choked back the welling tears in his eyes. Mason cupped her hand over her mouth and closed her eyes tight—pushing tears out from them. Orfa was turned away as she shook her head to herself. She blamed herself for not getting there in time.. As Raizar's life drifted away, looked upon the giant crystal once more. It was the last thing he ever saw.

"Such brilliance..." he said as he smiled warmly. Then, his body went completely limp as he passed. After a short few moments, the great man that had been Captain Raizar was no more. His spirit had left his body and vanished into thin air like an unseen vapor. The others broke down and wept profusely, mourning their dear friend and leader. It was around this time that the Steel Qobold's pilot, Ingram (a long-black-haired and thin fellow) landed the *Duchess* on top of the tower and ran over to meet them.

"Where's Fern and Erd?" he asked. Sloane, who was exhausted from having cleaned up the remaining undead, just shook his head slowly. Ingram seemed to sag in place when he heard this. To honor the three that were lost, they held a burial right then and there. Taking the bodies out of the castle, they buried them in the ground just outside it in three personal graves (Erd's being empty, of course, due to the nature of the Unwilling's Curse).

As the Vector Wolves stood above the mound of dirt that now covered up Raizar's grave (signified by his hat and revolver being placed above it), they each took a moment to reflect on their time with him. Sloane and Ingram did the same for Fern and Erd. Though Sonder had only known him for a short few days, the impact that Raizar had on him would last for the rest of his life. Maelo, who had returned to normal, whined, prompting Klay to kneel down and comfort him. "He's gone, bud. I know. But, it's going to be okay." Klay said, comforting the animal as he did his best to contain his emotions. "We got to know him at all, and that's what matters most." Klay added. Maelo looked up at him in that moment with profound sadness in his eyes before returning them to the sight of the grave.

Then, the rest of the Vector Wolves joined in on hugging Maelo. Even Orfa was there for the small animal, having to fight through her instincts, which normally told her to keep her distance from others. When their tears had dried, the Vector Wolves stood and walked past the captain's burial site to a cliff, where they stopped and looked up at the sight they had been rewarded with after all their struggling. For a quiet moment, they just enjoyed it all.

The crystal's light, its warmth, and the sense of pride they felt from the achievement. Sloane walked over to Sonder and the others, and congratulated them. The light of the kiln was being reflected off of his metal visor. "Well, you kids did damn good today. I'm sure that Ozo,

Fern, and Erd are watching over us and are proud of what they gave their lives to help accomplish. This really was a pivotal moment, and to have been right here where it began, on the front lines? There's no better place to be." he said as he smiled and then turned to gaze upon the crystalline surface of the radiating kiln.

"I'm sorry about your team." said Klay. "Fern and Erd were good people. You guys helped us out even though you didn't have to. You didn't owe us a thing." he the went on to say. This made Sloane smirk. "Raizar wasn't the only one who knew about the knells. Matter of fact, all the captains of the entire resistance network know about that little secret. When he reached out to us about your discovery and to discuss joining in on a joint countermeasure venture, we showed up with bells and all as soon as we could. The cause meant a great deal to Fern and Erd, as it does to me and to

Ingram. It's like that hope we've always been searching for finally showed up. We didn't want to pass that up or have anyone take our spot." Sloane then said.

"We're glad to have you here with us. I mean, we weren't expecting much but just one team? Out of however many could have been here? Don't get me wrong, I'm glad you guys came, but, what would have happened if you didn't?" Klay then asked him. "Don't worry about all that. We came, that's what matters." Sloane said firmly. They were all quiet for a brief time after this.

"How do you see, by the way, man?" Klay asked Sloane bluntly, tearing the silence. This got a laugh out of Sloane, who took the visor off his head, revealing a pair of lively, crystal-blue eyes, and turned it around for Klay. "See? One-way metal." the spiky-haired man explained. This made the lot of them chuckle altogether.

"Seriously? You fought these things in pitch-darkness while wearing sunglasses?!" Klay asked, sounding shocked. "Yes, sir." Sloane said, smiling as he placed them back over his eyes and turned once again to look at the kiln as he smiled broadly. "I knew it'd be a sunny day in the morning, so I brought 'em."

"Uh, it's technically night-time, yeah? Since we're on the upside-down point part of this strange, floating rock?" Sonder asked, indicating the kiln's position in the sky. They were all somewhat speechless at this. Nevertheless, they had become far more determined since winning this victory. The curtain of midnight had been forcibly moved back for once.

Sloane then offered up a proposition. "If you're ever in need someone to lead you, come to me." With this, Sloane turned around and walked over to Ingram, who had been standing some distance behind them and observing the strange, glowing light gem in the sky. After giving him a tap on the shoulder to snap the pilot out of his entrancement, Sloane stood with him, and they both continued staring as they soaked in the magic-like solar power of the kiln. It felt good on their skin. The heaped-up mounds of bluish ash dissolved away under the light if the kiln like ice in sunlight.

Then, Jasper reached up and placed Raizar's hat onto Sonder's head and asked: "Where to next, *Captain Snow?*" Prompting a tired smile from the white-haired worker. It looked as though everyone was in agreement over the choice of new leadership. In one hand, he held the orange gem sword, and the blue gem dagger in the other. Sonder raised the weapons and crossed them before the kiln of radiance. The bladed weapons drank in the source of energy like plants take to sunlight, causing their runes to give off a gentle glow. He didn't have all the answers. He hadn't the first clue as to where this all would be going. But, one thing was for certain: Sonder had found where he belonged.

"To wherever the Vector Wolves are needed next." Sonder answered firmly, his indigo eyes gleaming as they all stared up at the crystalline light in the sky with a renewed sense of hope. Shoulder-to-shoulder, they stood strong and together in a world of welcoming warmth. They would carry the memory of those they lost and continue fighting as long as they lived.

Suddenly, a fleet of ships appeared through rifts above the worlds, and an open frequency transmission played out of the Vector Wolves' wrist-worn communications devices, tearing their attention away from the beauty before them as duty called them: "Team 9? This is *Lady Arliss*

Chessa, Fatal Magistral and *Sovereign Commander* of *Thirteen Winds.* We have much to discuss...." The proper-accented and old timey-styled voice was coming out of a flying, stone-brick castle with the name: "Wardium" emblazoned in white paint on its side.

END OF VOLUME I

Author's Afterword

The original germ of creation I experienced for this story was back in 2019 when I was working as a patient server at a hospital. I was strolling down the halls of the in-patient rooms when I was struck with a vivid daydream about an evil-looking space-faring knight with flaming eyes. This would eventually become the character of Dey-Ud-Mund (whose name was originally spelled Deadmund when I first came up with it).

It was almost like having an alien message communicated to my brain. I was unable to remove it from my mind, and this was something that felt incredibly real in the moment, as though I were transported mentally somewhere else for a brief time. I wasn't on any kind of mind-altering medications or drugs, I was simply just exhausted from a thirteen-hour work shift and using caffeine as a crutch to keep me going. Later that same week, I would dream up a crew of unlikely heroes that fought against this villainous helmeted character, as well as their ship and the world they inhabited, which was a sci-fi space world with fantasy trappings.

For years going forward, I would frequently see these characters and their struggles in my head at each job I had until, at some point, I realized that these characters and this world had come to me in the form of mental flashes (spurred on likely by boredom and the need to occupy my mind while performing the rhythmic, rudimentary tasks of everyday work) so that they could be put into a story by my hands. At least, that's how I see story creation; the subconscious mind pushing an author or artist to make something of the flashes it shows the conscious mind.

I would attempt this countless times, each with a similar result of me not being confident in my ability to properly communicate what I was seeing in a way that made sense. Over time, however, I noticed a continual improvement of my writing capabilities until I hit a critical point of development in late 2023, when I finally felt as though I was ready and that the story had matured with me enough for it to see a public release. This was the result of me passionately throwing myself at something for several years without quitting and without any prior experience or training. Just simply going for it and dusting myself off whenever I faltered or failed at it.

With enough persistence, anything is possible. Though the story might not make perfectly logical sense, that was never my intention. Fantasy is this liquid, brain-chemical thing that can definitely be rationalized but should never be fully understood. If it was, it would defeat the point of it being just that; *fantasy*. It is escapism at its finest. Though it was a struggle, I ultimately had a tremendously great time putting this together and I'm truly grateful that I got to do it at this time in my life. Writing has become a passion for me, and it's one that I don't see myself giving up on anytime soon.

Thanks for checking out my little story and for giving it a chance! I sincerely hope you enjoyed it and are looking forward to what's coming next. At the end of all of this, that is all I truly want; for the stories I envisioned to be enjoyed by people.

I have to give credit where it's due:

To the many storytellers whose works and work ethics inspired me to sit down and make something of my own with the tools they had passed down to me.

To my English teacher back in high school for giving me the initial push I needed in order to start writing.

The biggest thanks, however, I give are to my dear friends and my mother, who continually encouraged me throughout my life to keep on chasing my dreams, no matter where they take me, and my father for challenging me at the right times. I am blessed to be their son, and to be able to show them a story I've written is truly a gift. I'm looking forward to showing

the world, my friends, and my family what I still have
left to tell.

This is just the beginning.

Take care now!

                                    - Mads

Database One:

Key Places, Races, and More

- The Maelstrom of Simult
  - The proper name for the multiverse containing all that is, was, and will be.
- Realms
  - The universes or planes of reality that exist within 'The Maelstrom.' There are thirteen of these within its bounds, as observed by Thirteen Winds Scouts.
- Floating Plateaus
  - The equivalent of planets and planetoids in Realm 13. They resemble upside-down mountains, with its inhabitable space

resembling a biome. Their rocky
bottoms are full of natural resources
and cave systems.
  - Examples include: Mythoss and
    Mortiss.
- Kilns of Radiance
  - Giant, magical crystals that are the
    equivalent of stars in Realm 13.
    These fuel the mortalforms of its
    bounds with *radiance*, a heat and
    light source derived from magical
    elements. A tightly-knit gathering
    of these giant crystals surrounds the
    tiny universe, this is referred to as
    'The Palisade of Radiance' which
    was used in the ancient past by the
    shapers of the realm to ward off
    Umbral powers and forces. It has
    been broken through and invaded by
    Ahz-Mund and his Unwilling.

(These hold a secret that will be explored in later volumes...)

- The Geleur
    - An extinct race of hyper-advanced, cyborg-like beings that is believed to have conquered and charted the Maelstrom of Simult in ancient celestial times. They disappeared some time ago due to unknown reasons.

- Umbral Beasts
    - Creatures born of the dark spaces between the realms. They are exclusively hostile towards any and all forms of life, sentient or no. Though weak on their own, these beings possess the bodies of mortalforms and bacterial life in order to maliciously influence the

events within the bounds of the
Maelstrom.

- Humans
  - The most common form of sentient
    mortalforms that have developed
    across the Maelstrom of Simult.
    Whether by design or by
    coincidence, they are all around
    similar levels of technological,
    cultural, and linguistic development.
    Their languages are universal across
    the realms. Though they are usually
    classified under two prominent
    biological genders, this line becomes
    blurred after enough development of
    the population and the idea of
    individuality, with some male
    members of the race exhibiting
    feminine qualities and vice-versa, as
    well as there being more of a fluid,

middle-ground. Each individual of this species has a name, family history, and traits derived from their genetics, cultural background, and raising. These beings live close to one-hundred years, with some even pushing it closer to one-hundred and fifty.

- Guardsmen
  - A space-faring race of humanoids that utilized Geleur technology in order to push back against the umbral forces under Ahz-Mund's control. They bear a striking resemblance to medieval knights found in a handful of the realms.
- Tech-Mages
  - Cohorts of the Guardsmen that are devoted to the study and utilization of radiant and umbral magicks and

technology. In appearance, they are much akin to wizards, sorcerers, and druids.

- Saurossians
  - ○ Hyper-evolved reptilian humanoids with a knack for bloodshed and savagery that have a pair of crystal-like rocks for eyes atop their heads. Hunting mostly for sport, these beings are solely driven by their need for violence and lust. They steal as opposed to inventing technology.

- Thirteen Winds
  - ○ A resistance network set in place by the Tech-Mages with the goal of spreading the discovery of the Rift Keys to those who will join their cause of finding a way to push back against Ahz-Mund's Unwilling

and/or locating a realm safe from the necromancer's clutches.

- o Examples include: the Vector Wolves and Steel Qobolds.

- Mund Dynasty
  - o The name given by Thirteen Winds to describe the main line of controllers that hold power over the Unwilling forces.
  - o Examples include: Ahz-Mund, Dey-Ud-Mund, and Mund-Karr-Mudgeon.

- Vector Wolf
  - o A race of dog-like creatures with three tails that is native to a world that the crew of the *Nameless Maiden* encountered and rescued. It is a loving glob of solid liquid that can split up into dozens and even hundreds of copies of itself before

the eyes of other mortalformic life. The natural benefit of this evolutionary trait is unknown. Though typically feral, these beasties can be domesticated into becoming "good boys."

- The Yarggen Clan
  - A tribe split down the middle by a civil war and scattered throughout the thirteen realms, these ferocious, beast-like individuals, who are marked by the tattoo striping that goes throughout their entire bodies, are adopted into said clan by proving their prowess in combat and in showcasing the survival skills they have learned and honed. While some genetic bloodlines exist within the clan, it is almost exclusively an amalgam made up of unique

individuals. Their population number and exact whereabouts are currently unknown, leaving Orfa as the sole, known member.

- Fates
  - Believed by Captain Raizar and many others to be the creators of the Maelstrom of Simult, these ethereal beings have omnipotent and omniscient dominion over all that was, is, and shall be. They control, influence, and manipulate the very threads of the multiverse they made down to a microcosm of size for truly unknowable reasons. It is beyond the capacity of most mortalforms to fully grasp their existence or even commune with them. But, this has happened before in the ancient past, hence how

civilizations learned of them in the first place.

Database Two:

Weapons, Technology, and Vehicles

Weapons

- Knell(s)
    - Mysterious weaponry created by the Geleur to fight Ahz-Mund. Has radiance properties that allow it to be duplicated by its wielder in order to arm legions at a time. Its malleability allows it to be transformed into different shapes.
- Dirge
    - An altar-like device used in combination with a knell to create a blast of destructive radiance energy.
- Elegy

- o A powerful, concentrated blast of radiant energy that comes from a combined dirge and knell. It can subdue any and all forms of umbral power.
- Guns
  - o Ranged weapons that propel bullets or shells from specialized magazines or clips to deliver damage from afar.
  - o Examples include: Raizar's revolver, and Klay's (stolen) Saurossian plasma repeater.
- Swords, Axes, Hammers, Clubs, and More
  - o Solid melee weapons used in place of ranged ones by humanoid mortalforms. Oftentimes, Ahz-Mund's Unwilling are equipped only with these, as he has no means of manufacturing bullets for his war

effort due to his use of zombified sentient beings.

Technology

- Radiance Runes
  - A source of magic-based energy used to power Geleur technology and weapons.
- Vapor
  - Super-heated water used in the propulsion systems of the resistance's ships. It rarely needs replacing due to the way it is recycled throughout the system.
- Plasma
  - Extremely hot bolts of semi-solidified gel that are utilized much like bullets.

Vehicles

- The Artoum
  - A Geleur floating fortress uncovered and utilized by the very last of the Guardsmen and Tech-Mages during their escape from Ahz-Mund.

- The Wardium and The Triennium
  - The two other floating fortresses that were under the control of the Guardsmen during their final hour, they closely tailed the Artoum until the very end. The fate of these crews is unknown. However, they are presumed dead (or undead, rather).

- The Nameless Maiden
  - Passed down through the generations of the Vohldt family line, this special vessel is home to

the Vector Wolves crew and has helped speedily get them to safety on numerous occasions. Could really use some detail work and a new coat of paint, though!

- Saurossian Dreadnought
    - An enormous, melded collection of scrapped and rusted over ships that the Saurossians stole from their victims that somewhat resembles a giant shark. The blood of those they take captive for food and sport is used like paint to decorate its haunting exterior.
- The Duchess
    - Sloane Sinclaire's ship. Used by the Steel Qobolds crew, who are under his command.

THE REALMS OF THE MAELSTROM

*Currently Designated by number

(Conquered Worlds are greyed out)

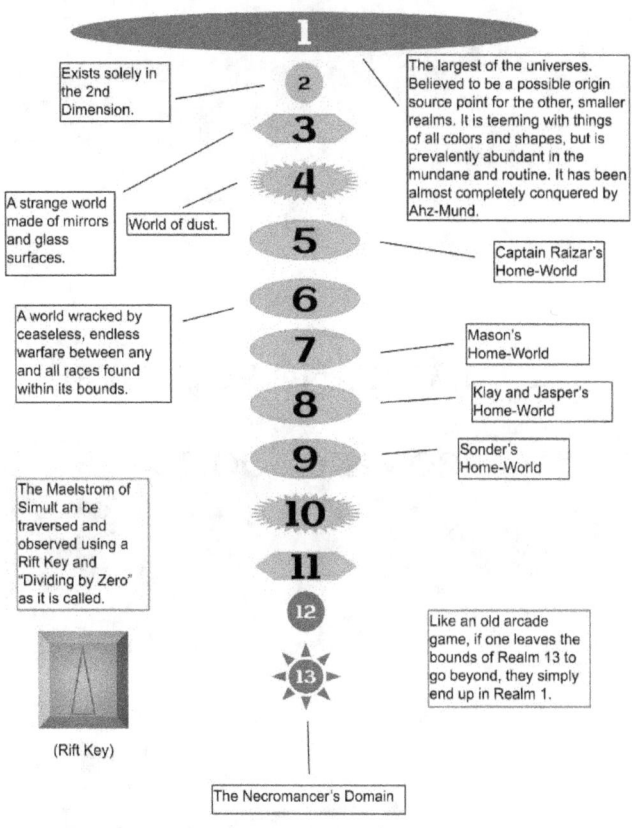

2 — Exists solely in the 2nd Dimension.

1 — The largest of the universes. Believed to be a possible origin source point for the other, smaller realms. It is teeming with things of all colors and shapes, but is prevalently abundant in the mundane and routine. It has been almost completely conquered by Ahz-Mund.

3 — A strange world made of mirrors and glass surfaces.

4 — World of dust.

5 — Captain Raizar's Home-World

6 — A world wracked by ceaseless, endless warfare between any and all races found within its bounds.

7 — Mason's Home-World

8 — Klay and Jasper's Home-World

9 — Sonder's Home-World

The Maelstrom of Simult an be traversed and observed using a Rift Key and "Dividing by Zero" as it is called.

13 — Like an old arcade game, if one leaves the bounds of Realm 13 to go beyond, they simply end up in Realm 1.

(Rift Key)

The Necromancer's Domain

VOLUME II AND VOLUME III

COMING SOON...